THE CRONE OF ELDERS BLAZE

IRIS BEAGLEHOLE

I

DELIA

Delia smiled to herself as delicious aromas filled the house. With Marjie's help, she'd found the little button on the oven that allowed it to be magically extended for special baking occasions, and of course, Christmas dinner. Now, the scent of multiple traditional meals were wafting through the cottage.

Kitty was in the kitchen, chopping lettuce. "I still can't believe we were all fooled," she said for the sixtieth time that day. "I mean, we all knew Jerry was terrible, but *that* terrible?"

Delia looked out the front windows of the house. Gillian would be arriving any moment with the children. She couldn't wait to see them.

She and Kitty had been cooking most of the day, preparing enough food to feed them all for a week, which was just as well, because after all that effort, she wasn't planning on lifting a finger for quite some time.

She turned back towards the kitchen and smiled at her best friend.

"Get over here, you lazy bones, and make me a cocktail," said Kitty as she tossed the salad.

Delia smiled to herself as she sloshed the Christmas margarita mix that Marjie had given her into the cocktail shaker with ice and began shaking it before pouring out the ruby-coloured liquid. The scent of cranberry and spices added to the already festive cheer.

"I hope they're not late," Delia said, glancing towards the window again as she passed Kitty her drink. "I wonder if they'll even be able to find the place. Gillian insisted she has no problems with using the map apps, like I do, but Myrtlewood is protected. I might have to go out on a bit of a hunt for them, bring them back."

Kitty sighed. "At least give them another ten minutes. Anyway, back to what I was saying before – Jerry bamboozled us all."

"Yes, I'm well aware of that," said Delia, although she was still reeling from the idea that her ex-husband of thirty odd years was also somehow one of the leaders of a ridiculous patriarchal secret society the whole time.

"It's funny. I kind of thought of the lot of them as buffoons, those red-cloaked maniacs..."

"And that's also how you thought of Jerry," said Kitty.

"When they first started sending those loons after you, you assumed it was Jerry and a theatre troupe."

"How close I was to the truth then..." Delia sighed and took a large swig of her drink, before thinking twice. She put the glass down in case she needed to drive soon, in search of her daughter.

"How's the divorce going, anyway?" Kitty asked.

Delia shrugged. "I haven't heard anything, recently, but I've got another meeting with the lawyer soon. The only problem is that Jerry seems to have disappeared, and even my excellent lawyer can't seem to locate him or his solicitor."

"Perhaps that's a good thing," said Kitty. "Good riddance."

Delia shivered. "The whole situation creeps me out. I wish the whole divorce was over and done with, but it can't be if Jerry is incommunicado. I don't think a judge will take kindly to 'please settle this now because my ex-husband is too busy leading a magical cult to uphold his side of the negotiations.' Of course, I'd rather not have anything to do with Jerry at all, but I'm not going to walk away from the house and everything I helped to build. It wouldn't be right."

"No, and I won't let you," said Kitty, patting Delia on the shoulder. "What are you going to tell Gillian?"

Delia grimaced. "I've been trying not to think about that at all. A bit much, isn't it? She's already been through a lot of changes lately. She's been so helpful, despite everything. You know, she even hired a private investigator to help me with the divorce case."

Kitty nodded. "Yes, you've told me that a few times."

"What am I supposed to say to her now? 'Oh, Gillian, by the way, your father...well it turned out the reason he was so distant and piggish was because he was really in a secret magical cult the whole time.'"

"I can see how that might not go down so well. Perhaps you could wait a bit."

"I don't know," said Delia. "I mean, Gillian deserves to know the truth. And what if she goes off to spend some time with him or sends the grandkids to him next?"

Kitty raised an eyebrow. "Perhaps you can warn her in a coded way that he's been mixed up in some sordid dealings. Maybe your lawyer could even back you up. He understands the magical world, doesn't he? When do I get to meet the handsome fellow?"

"My lawyer is in a committed relationship with a powerful witch," said Delia. "And by the way, you're also involved with someone."

Delia was just about to put on her coat and go in search of the main road to help Gillian get to Myrtlewood when the doorbell rang.

She heard a bark sounding from the front door.

"I bet I know who this is," Delia said with a smile. She opened the door and knelt down as a little beagle puppy rushed straight into her arms. "Where have you been hiding,

Torin?" she asked her familiar, scratching him behind the ears. He gave her a happy yip and licked her face.

During the winter solstice, when Delia and the other crones had gone off on their swamp mission, she'd sent this little guy to look after Kitty, which he'd done dutifully. He'd stayed at Una and Ashwyn's house, taken Kitty for walks, and then promptly disappeared.

Delia had wondered, with a pang of sadness and longing, whether he'd given up on her, but here he was again. He was just in time for Christmas, and as the car pulled up out front with three familiar faces staring in through the open door, so were Gilly and the grandkids.

"You found the place alright?" said Delia, as Gilly got out of the car. "I was just about to go out on a search and rescue mission."

Little Merryn ran up the steps and into Delia's arms, and even littler Keyne held his mother's hand and looked around as they approached.

"It's a difficult place to find, isn't it?" Gillian said. "You know, it's funny. I was about to call you and ask for more directions when this little puppy showed up. It was the strangest thing. I yelled at him to get out of the road and he ran ahead. The children begged me to follow along, and lo and behold, he led me to you!"

"Such a good puppy," Merryn cried, hugging him. "Is he yours, Nana?"

"It seems I'm looking after him – for the time being," Delia mumbled, not sure what else to say. The puppy shot her a disapproving look.

Gillian shook her head. "Strange thing to do, Mum. You run off to a weird little town. All of a sudden, you have a house and a pet."

"It seems like you're settling down, Nana," Keyne said, coming forward to hug Delia and plant a wet kiss on her cheek as she bent down awkwardly to greet him.

Delia straightened up, checking her back. It was far less achy than it used to be. Perhaps hanging out with those Crones had been good for her, or maybe it was just another feature of Marjie's special tonic. She made a note to ask.

"This is a special place, Nana," said Keyne.

Delia smiled at him. "It is a special place."

Merryn laughed. "Yes! It's magic."

Gillian raised an eyebrow. "I have to say, the house is adorable," she added as they entered the cottage.

"Thank you," said Delia. "I must admit it's rather strange, isn't it? I find myself so settled here already. But at least I'm close to you now."

"I'm terrified she's going to make it permanent," said Kitty, coming forward from the kitchen to give Gilly a peck on the cheek. "Ah, Gillian, so lovely to see you, darling. It's been far too long. Delia tells me you've gotten rid of that despicable husband of yours."

Gillian smiled tensely. "Yes, I might have," she mumbled. "It's been a strange time for all of us, I imagine."

"Indeed," said Kitty, giving Delia a stern look. They'd

promised not to mention magic in front of Gillian and the children.

Delia had had a hard enough time convincing her daughter that she wasn't going totally insane after all the strange occurrences that had happened to her in recent weeks. The last thing she needed now was to be institutionalised from a slip of the tongue.

"It smells delicious, Mum," Gilly said, although her face was scrunched up as if she was in some kind of pain. "What is it, love?" Gilly shook her head and waved her hand dismissively. "Oh, nothing. I just...I've got cramps."

"Proof that the gods are off their rocker," said Kitty, handing Gilly a cocktail.

Gillian shrugged and thanked her. "I can't drink very much. I have to leave tonight."

"Really. I've got the guest room made up for you too," Delia said, her heart falling.

"Sorry, Mum," said Gilly. "I have some important stuff that I need to do. I'll tell you about it at some point. I just...I just need to process. But thank you so much for taking the kids for a while."

Kitty sighed and Delia tried not to show her disappointment.

"I knew I wouldn't have you for long," Delia said gently. "I do wish it would be at least one night. Is that new law firm of yours working you to the bone?"

"No, it's not that," Gilly said. "I just can't talk about it yet, it's confidential."

Delia rolled her eyes. "Even from your own mother?"

"I'm afraid so," Gilly said.

Delia promptly decided to stop pouting and get on with setting the dinner table. "At least I've got the grandkids for a couple of weeks," she said, smiling at Merryn, who beamed back at her.

"We're going to have a great time, Nana. It will be extra-magic and there will be lots of amazing adventures and even some goats!"

"You say the funniest things, my love," said Delia, reaching out to stroke a golden tendril of hair behind his ear.

"So charming," Kitty agreed.

"Do you have much planned for the holidays?" said Gillian.

Delia and Kitty glanced at each other.

"Maybe some sightseeing," said Delia. "I suspect it might be too cold to go to the beach."

"Perhaps on a fine day," said Kitty. "There are lots of little pockets of the town to explore."

Kitty had done a bit of exploring over the past few couple of days, though it was largely focused on skincare from the Apothecary and sampling local beverages at the pub.

"You will be careful, won't you, Mum?" said Gillian, her voice tense.

"Of course, I will. I wouldn't risk anything happening to the children," Delia assured her.

"I know," said Gilly. "But I've heard strange things about this place." She looked around the room as if able to somehow assess the nature of the town from where she sat.

Delia noticed how pale her daughter's complexion seemed; her mind began to race with horrible thoughts. Gilly had barely touched her dinner.

Of course, she must be sick with some kind of terrible illness that she is not ready to talk about; that explains the confidentiality.

Delia's thoughts veered into increasingly panicked territory, wondering if perhaps Jerry was behind this. Could he have somehow poisoned their daughter just to get back at Delia? The possibility made her blood run cold. And yet, it was somehow even worse if Gillian had a regular old illness; at least something magical could have a magical cure. But for other ailments, she really had no idea, and she couldn't exactly ask Gillian about it now, not when she and Kitty had promised not to mention magic. Delia had half a mind to run off to find Marjie straight away to ask her what to do about her daughter, but that would have to wait.

Delia took a mouthful of stuffing and felt a pang of guilt. She'd been so annoyed with Gillian for creating so much distance between them; it had broken her heart to think they might lose their closeness. She'd been selfish. She had been through a lot lately; her marriage had broken down, so she had found herself a single, working mother and had to uproot her whole family for work...plus whatever confidential thing that had taken her colour and appetite, and Delia hadn't even been able to be there for her. She'd been so wrapped up in her own ridiculously dangerous adventures that she'd barely put any effort into figuring out how to help her daughter. Perhaps if she'd been more attentive, Gillian would have confided in her...

And then there was the other problem, of course. Gillian deserved to know about her father, and yet how could Delia tell her, especially where all the magic was concerned?

Delia was doing her best not to be thought a raving lunatic, but the effort was a tremendous strain.

"Have you heard from your father lately?" Kitty asked.

"Uh...no?" said Gillian, taken aback. "Why?"

Delia nudged Kitty with her foot, but she merely waved a dismissive hand and continued.

"I heard he's been caught up in some dodgy dealings," Kitty said, giving Delia a meaningful look.

Gillian frowned. "I last heard he was in London."

"You're not seeing him for Christmas?" Delia asked, her breath catching in her throat.

"Oh no," said Gillian. "I'm far too furious. It's sad how he's treated you, Mum. I'm not about to play happy families with him. Don't worry."

Delia breathed a quiet sigh of relief. "Good, best if you stay away for the time being, I think," she said, turning to the table as Gillian shot them both confused looks.

"What's this all about? Dodgy dealings?"

"Oh, nothing, dear. It's just..."

"Oh, yes," said Kitty, cutting in, "gangs, perhaps mafia, that sort of stuff."

"That's dreadful," said Gillian.

"I mean, that's only a rumour," Delia added hastily, not wanting to totally freak her daughter out.

"Best to steer clear for now," said Kitty.

"Agreed," Gillian replied, and Delia felt her shoulders relax a little.

Kitty, for all her overt enthusiasm, had done a good job steering Gillian away from her father. Though it might seem like a white lie, it wasn't all that different from the truth, leaving out the magic. She was merely suggesting the mafia instead of a secret brotherhood of musty monks who were nonetheless a dangerous gang of sorts.

The children enjoyed several helpings of Kitty's trifle, then leapt up from the table and raced around the room demanding presents which they enjoyed gleefully until Delia insisted it must be bed time.

Merryn sighed dramatically. "Why does it always have to be bedtime?" she asked, with a hand on her hip.

"Don't test me, young lady," said Delia, with a half-smile. She had to admit, she admired the girl's confidence.

"Bedtime is a great time of day," said Keyne dreamily, "because we get bedtime stories."

"I do like stories," Merryn admitted, giving her brother a playful shove.

"Alright, stories in five minutes," Delia announced. "If you can race into your pyjamas and brush your teeth that fast."

"I can, I can!" said Merryn. They ran off, with Keyne following close behind.

"I suppose I'd better go now," said Gillian. "I've got something first thing in the morning."

"It seems so dreadfully unfair," Delia said. "I know Christmas is often like this in modern families – and the children already had a special lunch with their father's family, but I do wish you could stay a little longer."

Gillian shrugged. "I kind of wish I could stay, too, but I'm afraid I can't..."

Delia smiled. "Well, I'm just happy to see you, and I'm so glad you made it for dinner."

Delia hugged Gillian but held a hand on her shoulder, making her pause before she could make her way out the door. "Look, darling, I know there's something you're not telling me. I just want you to know that, whatever it is, when you're ready to talk, I'm here. I don't care how scary it is."

Gillian looked taken aback. She stumbled over her words for a minute before allowing her shoulders to slump. "What do you think it is?" she asked suspiciously.

Delia shrugged. "I don't know, but you're so—"

"Mum—"

"Look, I'm not pressuring you to talk before you're ready," said Delia. "All I know is, after the last few weeks, I'm very open-minded to unusual things."

"That's sweet, Mum. But I'm not coming out of the closet or anything."

Delia laughed. "Darling, I used to work in the theatre. Queerness is hardly unusual. In fact, quite the opposite."

"Used to?" Gillian said. "So you've really given up your whole career because of that awful man?"

Gillian and her father had long had a strained relationship leading to far worse ways of referring to him.

Delia shrugged. "For now. Let's just say, I'm on a sabbatical before I figure out what to do when I grow up, but back to you..."

Gillian sighed. "I do want to talk. I really do, but I can't yet."

"It's okay," Delia said reassuringly, patting her daughter on the shoulder. "I'm here when you're ready."

After another hug was shared between them, and several farewells, Delia watched her only daughter wander out the front door, get into her car, and drive off into the night.

2
MARJIE

Marjie rocked gently in her chair, the motion harmonising with the crackling fire in the grand hearth of Thorn Manor. The living room was aglow with the warmth of Christmas, the air filled with the rich scent of spiced hot chocolate. The chaos of the past few days, particularly the harrowing events surrounding the winter solstice, seemed like a distant storm now calmed.

Rosemary Thorn lounged on the sofa, her red hair catching the light of the flames. Her vampire boyfriend, Perseus Burk, sat protectively close. Athena, Rosemary's teen daughter, was curled up in an armchair, her eyes reflecting the dancing flames.

Marjie took a sip of her hot chocolate, the spices tingling on her tongue, and let out a contented sigh. There was a cocoon of safety and warmth.

"You know," Rosemary said, breaking the comfortable silence, "I never thought I'd see Thorn Manor standing again after what happened."

Marjie nodded. "It's nothing short of a miracle." Her eyes glanced around at the restored grandeur of the manor.

Burk raised his glass in a toast. "Indeed, it was as if the very essence of the manor fought back against its destruction. It's more than just a house; it's a living part of magical history."

Marjie smiled at the thought. The manor, indeed, had become a character in its own right in the legends of the town. "It's more than just walls and floors; it's a guardian in its own way," she mused.

"The power that surged through here during the solstice was unlike anything I've ever felt," Athena added.

As the conversation lulled, Marjie's gaze lingered on the fire, watching the flames flicker. The warmth on her face was a stark contrast to the chill that had settled outside. She could hear the wind howling faintly beyond the walls of Thorn Manor, echoing a reminder of the wild magic that had recently swept through their lives.

Burk, his eyes reflecting the deep wisdom of centuries, spoke softly. "It's remarkable how quickly things can change. One moment everything is on the brink of collapse, and the next, it's as if a new chapter has begun."

"Yes," Marjie agreed, feeling the weight of his words. "Life is all about change. The solstice was a reminder of that."

Athena tilted her head, her eyes thoughtful. "This manor, our lives, they're all part of a greater cycle. I can feel it."

Marjie smiled, appreciating the wisdom in her words. She thought about the journeys they had all taken, the fears they had faced, and the courage they had found. "We've all been through so much," she said. "But here we are, together. That's what matters."

The fire crackled and Marjie felt a sense of peace settling over the room. The chaos of the past was behind them, and the future, though uncertain, seemed a little brighter with the hope of rekindling her own lost family ties. She looked at her companions, her friends, her chosen family, and felt a deep sense of gratitude. No matter what the future held, this was what mattered. She took another sip of her spiced hot chocolate, savouring it, along with the cheer of good company.

Athena, her eyes twinkling, looked across and said, "So, Burk, any ancient vampire secrets for surviving family gatherings? You've had, what, a few centuries of experience?"

Burk chuckled, a deep, melodious sound. "Ah, the secret is simple: always sit nearest to the exit and never, ever get into a debate over the best century for music."

Rosemary playfully nudged him. "And here I thought it was your charming personality that did the trick."

Marjie chuckled. "And let's not forget the most important rule: never run out of wine. Or in our case, hot chocolate."

"Speaking of which," Athena said, raising her empty mug with a grin, "I believe a refill is in order." She stood up to fetch the hot chocolate pot and refill their drinks.

Marjie leaned back in her chair, a contemplative look crossing her face as she listened to the gentle banter around her. "You know," she began, her voice soft but clear in the warmth of the room, "as a witch, I never put much stock in celebrating Christmas in the traditional sense. It always seemed a bit...disconnected from my own practices."

She took a thoughtful sip of her hot chocolate, savouring the rich, spicy flavour. "But over time, I've come to appreciate the magic of this season, the way it builds on the old traditions of Yule and transforms them. Yes, there's a lot of...what's the word..."

"Consumerism?" Athena offered.

"Indeed," Burk agreed.

"That's the one!" said Marjie. "Sure there's all the pressure for shopping and meaningless rubbish in how people think they're supposed to celebrate it. But there's also something deeper, something that resonates with the old ways."

Marjie's gaze drifted to the fire, watching the flames as they crackled. "It's about the gathering of energy, the communal spirit that sweeps across the country, and indeed, the world. There's a power in that, a kind of magic that might be different from what I practice, but magical all the same."

She looked around at the smiling faces of Rosemary, Athena, and Burk. "I might not follow the Christian traditions."

"Or the corporate ones," Rosemary added.

Marjie smiled at her. "No, but there's something undeniably special about family time, sharing good food, laughter, and the exchange of thoughtful gifts. It's a celebration I can wholeheartedly get behind."

Rosemary smiled warmly at Marjie's words, the flickering

firelight reflecting in her eyes. "I think that's beautifully put, Marjie," she said. "Christmas, Yule, or whatever we choose to call it, it's a time when we can all find common ground. It's about the heart, not the labels we put on things."

Athena grinned. "It's like we're all tapping into the same story, but just telling it in our own ways. And it's cool how we can blend our traditions to create something unique."

Burk nodded in agreement. "Yes, the essence of these celebrations transcends time and belief. As someone who's seen many a winter, I can attest that the joy of togetherness is a constant, no matter the era or the culture."

"And let's not forget the food!" Rosemary chimed in with a laugh. "Good food is a universal language of its own. It's one tradition that everyone can agree on."

Athena grinned. "Totally! I'm stuffed. And I have to admit, the presents aren't too bad either, even if it's just little things. It's more about the thought and the fun of giving."

Rosemary looked around the cosy room, decked in literal boughs of holly and other gorgeously festive decorations, a soft smile on her lips. "I must say, Thorn Manor does Christmas quite well. It's like living in a Christmas card."

Marjie nodded in agreement. "Yes, except our card includes witches, a vampire, and a magical house. Not your typical festive fare."

Athena raised her refilled mug. "To an atypical but wonderful family," she toasted.

"To family," they all echoed, clinking their mugs together, the sound mingling with the laughter that filled the room.

As Marjie looked around at the smiling faces of those she now considered family, her thoughts drifted to other dear friends like Papa Jack who were safely ensconced in their own houses, then her mind wandered further afield to her estranged brother in Yorkshire. The sense of closeness she felt here made her wonder about him. What was his life like now? Perhaps it really was time to reconnect, to bridge the gap that time and circumstances had widened.

She took another sip of her chocolate, the warmth spreading through her. "You know, I've been thinking about trying to call my brother again. It's been too long, and life's too short for regrets."

Rosemary reached out and gave Marjie's hand a reassuring squeeze. "I think that's a wonderful idea, Marjie. Family ties, no matter how strained, are worth mending – unless they're toxic, of course."

Marjie nodded, feeling both of apprehension and hope. The night was peaceful, a balm after the storm. In this moment, at least, she felt ready to face whatever lay ahead.

3
DELIA

Merryn and Keyne raced back down the stairs in their pyjamas, demanding stories.

Delia took one last swig of her cocktail.

"I'll get on with the dishes then, shall I?" Kitty suggested, getting up. "You've got more important things to do."

"If you don't mind," Delia said. "I'll join you soon."

"Don't make promises you can't keep," Kitty replied. "Storytime has no bounds."

"Indeed." Delia chuckled, following the children back upstairs.

The attic space of the cottage had long been converted into a children's bedroom, complete with twin beds. Perhaps the previous owner had grandchildren or perhaps it was from when Liam was little. Either way, it made for a delightful room for her own family's purposes.

Merryn and Keyne seemed to think so too.

"I've got the bed with the bunny sheets," Keyne told her enthusiastically.

"I'm too old for bunny sheets," Merryn added, with a serious tone. "Mine have unicorns."

"As it should be," said Delia, smiling. "Now, what story are we having?"

Delia used theatrical voices, much to her grandchildren's delight. She proceeded through several rounds of Christmas books. She had bought them a lot of the classics, unsure what else to get in a magical town like Myrtlewood. She read several Beatrix Potter stories about Peter Rabbit, a few *My Naughty Little Sister* tales, and once Keyne had drifted off to sleep, Merryn requested a chapter of *The Worst Witch*, her absolute favourite.

As they drifted off to sleep Delia tucked the books away and looked out the window, where gentle snow was falling.

Fortunately, the weather had returned to how it should be in winter. Recently, there had been a rather strange time as far as the climate in Myrtlewood was concerned. Delia thought she was losing her marbles when the bluebells started to bloom and woodland animals came out of hiding in late December.

She couldn't quite understand what had transpired and was unsure whether Rosemary and Athena were to blame or were heroes in the situation; perhaps they were both. After all, morality was often more shades of grey than black and white.

That thought led her, inexplicably, to picture Declan in her head – "the Cowboy", as she called him in her mind.

What was he doing now? Delia had the sense that he'd been stalking her, which was not a particularly pleasant thought. He seemed troubled in some indeterminable, ancient way.

There was an emptiness inside him; he was an enemy, and yet at times he'd warned her, even protected her and the other Crones from the Order of Crimson. Was this just another one of Jerry's games? Had he, too, been sent to seduce her the way that Jerry had been, or the way that the old legend about the witch being seduced by the dark mage had transpired all those centuries ago?

It was too confusing to figure out, a verifiable enigma. There was something charismatic and compelling about him. Clearly he was dangerous; he was certainly working for the Order, even if he sometimes worked against them. Still, Delia felt sure he was an enemy. Another trick to control her life.

Where was he now? Alone out there in the cold? As she looked out into the winter night Delia felt a sudden over-whelming sense of sorrow for him.

Closing the curtains, she couldn't shake the feeling she was being watched.

Returning downstairs, she found Kitty had already finished tidying up and was lounging in an arm chair with a fresh cock-tail by the fire.

"This is the life," Kitty said, raising her glass.

"You know how you get that feeling sometimes, like somebody's watching you?" Delia asked.

"Always, darling, I'm quite mesmerising." Kitty winked. "But I know what you mean," she added, giving Delia a look.

Delia merely sighed.

"I think it's normal to feel like that, don't you?" said Kitty reassuringly.

"Things haven't been very 'normal' at all, recently," said Delia. "And now, I just don't know what to believe anymore. I keep thinking about this man..."

"Oh, do tell," urged Kitty, intrigued.

Delia gave her friend a brief rundown of the cowboy and some of their various encounters.

"He sounds like a handsome stallion," said Kitty playfully.

"Handsome, certainly," Delia replied, gently giving her friend a nudge. "But dangerous."

"Now, don't go falling for some broken man who needs rescuing, Delia."

"I'm not about to do that," Delia insisted. "What makes you think he's a romantic interest at all?"

"Just the tone of your voice when you describe him," replied Kitty.

"He is intriguing," admitted Delia. "But how can I ever trust a man who's betrayed me over and over to the enemy?"

"Indeed," said Kitty, pouring another drink.

4

DECLAN

I n the dense, shadow-draped forest, Declan sat by a small fire, the flickering flames warming his weathered skin. The flames crackled softly. The forest was a sanctuary, alive with the chorus of nocturnal creatures. Above him, the canopy of trees swayed gently. The air was filled with the earthy scent of the damp forest floor, mingling with the smoky aroma from the fire.

He moved closer, kneeling beside his campfire. Before him, a small iron pot hung over the fire, suspended from a makeshift stand of branches. He began preparing his evening meal, a task that brought a semblance of calm to his otherwise tumultuous existence.

He laid out the ingredients he had foraged earlier in the day: wild herbs, roots, and a piece of game meat he had caught.

His thoughts drifted, again and again to Delia Spark, the

woman who had unwittingly reawakened a torrent of long-dormant emotions within him. At first, it was rage that burned in his chest – a fiery, consuming anger. But now, as he gazed at the forest around him, he saw it in a different light. The leaves seemed more vibrant, the night sounds more melodic. A new and old magic was stirring within him, awakening senses he thought had long since withered.

With a sharp knife, Declan deftly sliced the meat into chunks, his movements precise and practiced. The meat sizzled as it hit the hot surface of the pot, the sound a crisp counterpoint to the soft crackling of the fire. He watched as the pieces browned, turning them over to ensure they cooked evenly, their rich aroma wafting up and blending with the smokiness of the fire.

Declan's hands paused in their task as he pondered the contract on Delia, the sacred oath that bound him. He longed to escape it, but to break it would mean sacrificing his powers – everything except his insufferable immortality. His existence had been a relentless pursuit of distraction, his powers the only solace in an otherwise endless void.

He reached for the herbs and roots he had gathered. With a careful hand, he crushed the herbs between his fingers, releasing their fragrant oils. The scent of thyme and wild garlic filled the air, a reminder of the forest's bountiful offerings. He scattered the herbs into the pot, along with the roots, which he had chopped into small pieces.

As the stew began to come together, Declan poured in some water he had collected from a nearby stream. The liquid hissed as it hit the hot surface, steam rising and mingling with the cool evening air. He stirred the mixture slowly, watching as the ingredients began to meld together, the meat tenderising and the herbs infusing their flavour.

The simple act of cooking, something he had done countless times over his long life, felt different now. The forest around him seemed to be watching, its ancient trees witnesses to his inner turmoil.

The stew simmered softly and Declan's thoughts inevitably drifted again to Delia Spark. She was the cause of all this – the spark igniting his madness, the instigator of this untethered sensation, making him feel unbearably light, especially after the heavy burden of so many years. The emotions she had stirred in him were as complex and layered as the flavours developing in his pot.

Declan stirred it methodically, the spoon moving through the thick, hearty mixture with practiced ease. The stew was a simple concoction of game meat and wild herbs he had foraged from the forest – a meal born of necessity, not desire. The rich aroma of the stew filled the air, a blend of earthy and robust scents, but Declan's appetite was for something far more complex than the food before him.

As he added a handful of wild thyme to the pot, the herb's aromatic scent released into the steam, mingling with the smoky air. He watched as the leaves wilted, surrendering their essence to the stew. It was a small act, yet it reminded him of the intricate balance of life and decay, of taking and giving back, a cycle he had been part of for far too long.

He scooped a spoonful of the stew to taste, blowing gently to cool it. As he tasted it, the flavours of the forest exploded on his tongue – a reminder of the simple pleasures he had long forsaken.

It was in a dense and ancient forest, such as this, where the air was thick with the scent of moss and earth, many centuries earlier. The trees stood like silent sentinels, their branches swaying gently in a breeze that carried whispers of forgotten tales. The ground beneath his feet was soft, the soil rich and yielding, a stark contrast to the firm resolve in his heart as he sought something more than his mortal life could offer.

The trickster god appeared before him in a swirl of mist, a figure both awe-inspiring and terrifying. His presence filled the air with a charge, like the static before a storm. The god's eyes were deep pools of starlight, drawing Declan in, promising secrets of the universe and the allure of forbidden knowledge.

As the god spoke, his voice resonated not just in Declan's ears but in his very soul. It was a melody that promised power, a temptation that played upon Declan's deepest desires.

...Immortality

The word wrapped around him like a cloak, warm and seductive, lulling him into a sense of security and glory.

When the god extended his hand, a radiant energy emanated from his palm, casting an ethereal glow in the dim forest. Declan reached out, his heart pounding with anticipation. The moment their hands touched, a surge of power unlike anything he had ever felt coursed through him. It was a torrent of magic, wild and untamed, rushing into his veins, filling him with a euphoria that was both exhilarating and overwhelming.

But as quickly as it came, the sensation twisted. The euphoria turned to a searing pain, as if the magic itself was burning him from the inside. The god's laughter, dark and echoing, filled the clearing, a sound that would haunt Declan for centuries. He realised too late the deception, the curse hidden within the gift.

He could not die, and yet everything else did. Everyone else... everything he cared about...it all soon turned to dust, and yet, mundane in every other way, he had to forge on.

So many years passed, so many wars and losses and victories that all blurred together.

He had given up hope of goodness when the witch found him in that abandoned church.

She was a figure of ancient power, her presence commanding yet enigmatic. Her eyes held the depth of centuries, and when she spoke, her voice was like the rustling of leaves, a natural force that was both beautiful and formidable.

She spoke of a bond, a connection that would grant him access to the magic he craved, but at a price.

She wove her spell around him with words as old as the earth itself. Declan remembered the sensation of the magic binding him, a feeling like chains wrapping around his soul, pulling him into servitude and endowing him with powers that made his life more bearable...the ability to track, and to weave portals, but the gaining of these powers was a bittersweet experience, filled with the hard realisation of his new bondage.

It was a moment that defined his existence, a pivotal point where he gained everything and yet, somehow, lost even more. The witch's life had long been extinguished, but the oath he'd taken with his very blood in that dusty ruin bound him always to work, wherever he could find it, and to break such a contract would be to destroy the powers that kept him anchored in his long and solitary existence. A blessing and a curse.

He was jolted back to reality by the bubbling of his stew. After tending it in contemplation for many more long moments, it was ready. He ladled it into his bowl. The flavours were rich and hearty. Yet, as he ate, his mind was elsewhere, tangled in the web of yet newfound sensations.

His meal was interrupted by the flicker from his seer's stone. It glowed ominously beside him, breaking the tranquillity of the moment. It wasn't the Cleric this time. The image that materialised was of his superior, a man known only as The Shepherd, his eyes devoid of life, his smile cold and calculating.

5
DELIA

Delia had expected a small town like Myrtlewood would be closed around Christmas. However, to her surprise, when she went for a walk with the grandchildren and the dog the next morning – promising to bring Kitty back some coffee if she could locate any – she found everything seemed to be running as usual.

"I suppose the solstice is more of a big deal here," Delia mused to herself.

"What's that, Nana?" said Merryn.

"Oh, nothing. I was just talking to myself. You get to do that more and more as you get older. It's quite fun, really." She winked.

Merryn looked her straight in the eye. "You said something about the solstice. I've been learning about it at school. It's to do with the sun being in a certain position." Merryn pointed up at the bright orb hanging low in the sky. "In winter, it's on an angle – the *most* biggest of an angle, and then in summer, it's the opposite."

"You're very astute, my darling," said Delia, patting her on the head.

Delia wondered if Merryn and Keyne were affected by the witchy family powers that had caused Delia so much trouble recently. Was that what was going on with Gillian too? Was she going through some kind of magical episode, believing that she was actually losing her mind? Did Gilly leave on Christmas so soon because she feared setting them all on fire, or was it something else?

Delia sighed.

"What is it, Nana?" Keyne asked as they strolled along the street.

"Nothing, I just feel like I need to have a better conversation with your mother."

"Mum has been a bit weird lately," said Merryn.

"Oh yes?" Delia wanted to pry, but Merryn had already lost interest in the subject, and she didn't want to put her grandchildren in a position of telling on their mother.

"Look, a tea shop," said Merryn as they approached Marjie's.

Keyne frowned. "But you like coffee, Nana."

"I do," Delia replied. "And they also have coffee, here."

"I'll have tea," said Keyne proudly.

"Very well. Perhaps we should all have tea. And I'll have an extra coffee."

"And bring one back for Kitty," said Merryn primly.

"Oh yes, we'd better add some treats, don't you think?" Delia suggested.

"Treats!" the children exclaimed excitedly. They'd had had a simple breakfast of toast after their big dinner last night, so by now, they were clearly ready for more delicious things.

They entered the teashop and the children's eyes lit up in delight.

"I'd have thought you'd take some time off after the week you've had," Delia said as she greeted Marjie who promptly stepped out from behind the counter and gave Delia an enormous hug, then proceeded to do the same with the children, who greeted her as if they were old friends.

"I am so delighted to meet you both," Marjie said. "What wonderful young people you are! Now, what kinds of delicious things do you like?" She gestured to the cabinet.

Merryn and Keyne's eyes grew even wider as they took in all the cakes and pastries. They stepped closer to the counter, mesmerised.

"How are you holding up, my love?" Marjie asked quietly.

Delia shrugged. "It's wonderful to have them, really."

"But you're worried about your daughter, still, I can tell," said Marjie.

Delia nodded, checking that the children were far too busy choosing cake to overhear.

"Not to mention Gilly's father being what he is," Delia muttered.

Marjie smiled sympathetically. "You haven't tried to tell her, have you?"

Delia shook her head. "Definitely not."

"Well, these things have a way of working themselves out," said Marjie. "Stay the course and enjoy the moment."

"I would actually enjoy one of your famous scones right now," Delia admitted, "and the strongest coffee you can muster."

"Just your luck," said Marjie. "I've acquired an espresso maker."

Delia felt a thrill of excitement, which was quickly replaced by anxiety as she glanced at the complicated-looking contraption in the corner of the kitchen, which oddly seemed to be covered in knitted tea cosies.

"Erm…" Delia began. "I don't think you need to keep it warm like that."

"I'm still kind of working it out," Marjie admitted, "but I could probably rustle you up a cappuccino." She went out to the kitchen before Delia could protest.

Delia heard a few buzzing and humming noises and some subtle cursing, while she helped the children select their morning tea.

Merryn wanted a strawberry layer cake, and Keyne wanted chocolate.

"I'll put your orders through in a minute, when Marjie's back. For now, we can take a seat," said Delia, leading them over to the table. A moment later, Marjie bustled back with a cup piled high with frothed milk and cinnamon.

"A cappuccino, madam!" Marjie announced.

Delia's smile must have looked rather nervous.

"At least give it a try," said Marjie reproachfully.

"I will, and I'm sure it will be marvellous," Delia replied. She took a sip, finding the coffee drinkable enough, though rather too milky. She didn't dare mention it, not wanting to criticise her friend who was already feeling rather sensitive. "Delicious!" Delia said enthusiastically. "Now, children...tell Marjie what you want."

Merryn looked over to the cabinet. "I thought I wanted the strawberry one, but now I kind of want all of them."

She sighed wistfully.

"Me too," said Keyne. "And tea!"

"Ah, not to worry," said Marjie. "I'll whip you up a sampling platter...and how about I bring you a pot of my special Christmas tea?" She lowered her voice to a whisper and added, "Caffeine free," into Delia's ear.

Delia smiled. "That sounds brilliant."

Marjie returned moments later, bearing a tray full of tiny cakes. These weren't just little pieces; they were miniature replicas of the full-sized ones.

"Marjie!" said Delia. "You've certainly outdone yourself."

"These are magical cakes, I can tell," said Keyne.

Merryn nodded. "Yes, that's why we needed to sample them all."

Delia raised an eyebrow.

"Not to worry, dear," said Marjie. "Children understand these things."

"Oh yes, of course we understand magic," said Keyne.

He was so matter-of-fact that Delia wanted to believe him. Childhood tended towards the whimsical, after all – children often believed in things like the tooth fairy and Santa Claus, but it wasn't quite the same thing as what she'd experienced recently in blazes of fire. However, taking Marjie's lead, Delia decided to go along with it. "Well then, we're all going to have a magical time."

She smiled and bit into her scone, which was indeed an enchanting experience all on its own.

6

AGATHA

Agatha Twigg sat at her sunlit kitchen table, sharing a comfortable silence with her niece, Marla. The air was filled with the pleasant aroma of toast and butter.

Marla picked up the teapot and glanced across the table. "Would you like more tea, Aunt Agatha?"

Agatha looked up from her thoughts, a soft smile playing on her lips. "Yes, that would be lovely, thank you," she replied. "I'll be heading to my library shortly. There's some research I need to delve into."

Marla nodded, knowing well the deep connection her aunt had with her books.

Moments later, Agatha rose from her chair, feeling the familiar pull of her cherished books calling to her. With a grateful nod to Marla, she made her way to her library, ready to immerse herself in wisdom.

Agatha stepped through the door, inhaling the vanilla-scent of old books in this sanctuary of tomes. She had always felt at peace here. But now, something was amiss.

What is that breeze?

Her keen eyes scanned the room, searching for an open window that could be the source of the sudden draft. Yet, she found them all securely shut.

A frown creased her brow.

"What in Cerridwen's cauldron is going on?" she muttered, taking a step back as the wind within the room grew stronger, sending papers fluttering from her desk like a flock of startled birds.

She watched as the carefully organised notes on her desk took flight in a chaotic formation.

"This is absurd," Agatha said as a realisation dawned on her – it wasn't the windows, but her own burgeoning power at fault.

Her powers had been building ever since the winter solstice, when she and the other Crones had unlocked their ancient magic, but this was clearly getting out of hand. She felt suddenly very small, like a novice again or a child struggling to grasp the reins of a wild and unruly horse.

The books on the shelves began to vibrate, some teetering on the edge of falling. Agatha extended a hand, trying to will them into stillness.

"Stay put, you," she commanded sternly. But the books defied her.

She took a deep breath, trying to calm the storm within.

Her nerves had been frayed since the solstice, often feeling like she was trapped in a pressure cooker about to burst. "It's not you, my darlings," she said to her beloved books, her voice softening. "It's this blasted magic of mine."

The wind picked up further, and so did many of her precious books and papers.

The room now resembled the inside of a snow globe, with pages and parchment swirling around her.

"Aunty?" The voice cut through the chaos, causing Agatha to turn sharply.

Marla, balancing a tray laden with a steaming teapot and cups, cautiously stood by the library door. Books and papers continued swirling around the room like leaves caught in an autumnal gale.

"What in Herne's Horns is happening?" Marla exclaimed, her eyes wide with astonishment, carefully setting the tray down on the hall table outside.

Agatha suppressed her own embarrassment in finding herself so completely out of control. She attempted again to calm the whirlwind of literature with a wave of her hand.

"Are we under attack?" Marla asked, peering through the chaos as if looking for a library intruder.

"Oh no, Marla! It's just my...well, my magic."

"How absurd," Marla said flatly.

Agatha nodded, then turned her attention back to the unruly scene. "Enough now, settle down!" she commanded, but the books seemed to only twirl faster, as if in defiance.

Marla let out a nervous chuckle.

Agatha turned to Marla, a sheepish smile on her face. "I'm afraid tea might be a bit challenging under these circumstances."

Clearly, getting angry wasn't helping. Another approach was required here. After all, what was the point in being the Air Crone if she couldn't control the wind?

Agatha closed her eyes, focusing on the core of her being, where her power surged from. She held her hands to her ribcage and focused on calm sensations.

She imagined her power settling into a breeze, gentle and controlled, rather than this gale that now threatened to upend her sanctuary. The wind slowed.

Agatha opened her eyes, surveying the disarray.

"Enough," she whispered, her voice firm.

The whirlwind abated, the papers descending in a graceful ballet to the floor, the books tumbling to the floor.

Agatha sighed, surveying the mess. Her powers were a gift, but they were also a burden, especially when they misbehaved.

7
MATHILDA

Mathilda's gaze swept over the quaint town, taking in its rustic charm and the gentle hum of everyday life. She'd only ever been to Myrtlewood as a young child, in fact, she'd hardly been anywhere other than the Clochar of the Veiled Sisterhood and the small residence the sisterhood kept nearby as a safehouse. The unfamiliarity of this place stirred excitement and apprehension in equal measure. The world outside the sisterhood's high walls was so different, so vibrant and unpredictable.

Mathilda found herself amidst chaos. Cars, which she had seen from a distance on rare missions, now careened through the streets around her. She watched as a grumpy man in a small, bright red vehicle tried to park, its back end sticking out awkwardly. She mused with a wry smile. "It seems not all technology makes things simpler."

Moments later, she encountered a small group of teenagers with odd-coloured hair, their thumbs flying over the screens of their small rectangular devices. Mathilda observed them with curiosity and amusement. "Scrying devices for the modern age? How times have changed," she whispered to herself, thinking of the intricate and solemn rituals of scrying back at the Clochar.

Mathilda made her way discretely to the local public house, the Witch's Wort. She'd written to secure lodgings for her stay.

The pub, with its rustic hanging sign and inviting aroma, was rather different to plain white-washed buildings of the Clochar. The pub's charm was evident in its exposed wooden beams, walls adorned with quaint local memorabilia, and dim, warm lighting. For Mathilda, this created a surprisingly cosy and welcoming atmosphere. The murmur of conversations blended with the occasional hearty laughter.

A moment after entering, she was greeted by a woman with dark blonde hair and a warm smile.

Mathilda stumbled, unused to strangers. "I...err..."

"Welcome! You must be Mathilda. I'm Sherry. Your room is all ready for you," the woman said kindly, gesturing for her to follow.

Mathilda's eyes darted nervously towards the men in the pub, huddled around their table, hairy and causal. She had rarely encountered any men in all her life. She could feel their eyes on her as she passed, igniting a sense of vulnerability. *This is all so very strange.*

Reaching her room, Mathilda was relieved to find it clean

and comfortable, with a sturdy lock on the door that provided a sense of security.

Sherry left her there with a friendly reminder that she could ask for anything she needed.

Alone and in peace, Mathilda let out a deep breath before dutifully pulling out her black mirror. As she prepared to activate it, she paused, reflecting on her task.

She was here to convince the Crones to accept the Sisterhood's assistance, a task that seemed daunting amidst her own uncertainties. The Crones, especially her own sister, would not be easily swayed.

She whispered the familiar charm to activate the mirror. The surface swirled with shadowy tendrils before the faces of the elder sisters appeared.

"Mathilda, you've arrived safely," Sister Gwyneth said with a small, relieved smile.

"Yes, Sisters. I'm in Myrtlewood and will approach the Crones soon. I...I admit, this world is much different from what I've known," Mathilda confessed.

"Remember, Mathilda, the strength of the Sisterhood is with you. Trust in your training and in the wisdom we have imparted," Sister Breag advised.

Mathilda nodded, absorbing their words. The connection to the Sisterhood, though through a mere mirror, grounded her. She was no mere adventurer. She was here for a reason, her contribution was a small part of something greater, however daunting her role might seem.

Mathilda took a moment after the conversation to gather

her thoughts. She would meet the Crones, convey the Sisterhood's message, and navigate this strange outer world with dignity and strength, but first, she needed sustenance.

Mathilda's steps slowed as she re-entered the pub, the warm ambiance of the room enveloping her. As she took in the lively atmosphere, her mind wandered back to the serene corridors of her childhood, where the rhythm of life was dictated by ritual and discipline. The laughter and chatter around her hinted at sense of freedom unknown to her.

Life here thrives on an exhilarating chaos...

She sat down at an empty booth, scanning the menu filled with foods she remembered from her childhood – pies and chips and battered fish. Such rich meals were never served in the Clochar, and to indulge in them now seemed inappropriate. Sherry approached and Mathilda ordered the stew. It arrived moments later. The aroma was inviting, far more hearty than she was used to. It was saltier and more flavourful, each spoonful a delightful experience that warmed her from within.

Sherry, noticing her deep appreciation of the meal, approached again with a smile. "Enjoying your meal, love?" she asked.

"Yes, very much," Mathilda replied.

Encouraged by Sherry's friendliness, Mathilda retrieved a piece of paper from her pocket, her mission coming back into focus. "I'm trying to find these women, do you know them?" she asked, revealing the list of names.

Sherry glanced at the paper, her eyes briefly scanning the

pub. They paused momentarily on a silver-haired woman sitting beside a rugged, protective-looking man.

"I'm not in the business of giving out information on people around here," Sherry replied, her tone gentle yet firm.

Mathilda nodded, a bit disheartened but understanding the need for discretion. "No, it's fine. Thank you. I'll find them easily enough," she said, masking her disappointment with a smile.

Sherry gave a sympathetic nod and retreated, leaving Mathilda to glance back across to the silver-haired woman – Agatha!

She braced herself and approached the table. "Hello, Agatha Twigg? I'm here to offer help on behalf of the Sisterhood," she stated, her voice steady but her heart racing.

Agatha's eyes landed on Mathilda's face sparking in recognition. It was a good thing then, that she'd been the one in the safe house that night. She'd helped the Crones and now, with any luck, they'd trust her.

"What sisterhood?" the man asked gruffly, his posture protective.

Mathilda averted her gaze, feeling uneasy under the scrutiny of a man. "It's fine, Covvey," Agatha intervened with a dismissive wave. "Never you mind."

Mathilda seized the moment to speak directly to Agatha. "I've been sent to find you and offer assistance. The Sisterhood believes you and your companions are in need of our help."

Agatha's expression shifted from guarded to sceptical. "And

why would we need help from your Sisterhood? We manage just fine on our own."

Mathilda hesitated, choosing her words carefully. "We have resources, knowledge that could be beneficial to you. We believe there's a common cause that needs addressing."

Before Mathilda could continue, Agatha interjected sharply, "You should be talking to your own flesh and blood sister first. Isn't she the one you should be finding?"

Mathilda felt a pang of guilt at the mention of Ingrid. "I just arrived in town. I am planning to see her..."

Agatha shook her head, clearly not convinced. "Well, if you're looking for help, you're barking up the wrong tree. We're not interested."

Feeling the conversation slipping away, Mathilda tried again. "Please, just hear me out. There's more at stake here than you might realise." Mathilda held up a small brown pouch. "This is a special token from the Sisterhood. It will protect you."

But Agatha was resolute. "I think you've said enough. We can take care of ourselves. Goodnight."

Mathilda tried again to give Agatha the gift, only to be waved away dismissively.

She stood there for a moment, the sting of rejection biting at her, then she nodded silently and stepped away, unsure how to proceed. Her mission was too important to give up at the first hurdle. She had to find a way to reach out to these women, to bridge the gap between the Sisterhood's intentions and their scepticism. There was far more at stake than they realised.

8

DELIA

Delia was just finishing her second coffee when the telephone rang. The children were laughing and doing their best to play in the small amount of snow in the back garden, decked out in their gloves and hats, while she watched from the sunroom.

The last thing she wanted in that moment of peace and tranquillity was a phone call from Agatha. However, that's exactly what she got.

"Delia," Agatha's scratchy voice informed her, "your plans for the day are about to change. We're needed at Ingrid's house this afternoon."

"But the children and I were going to go and get hot chocolates," Delia replied, glancing back at the garden.

"The children?" Agatha seemed to sneer, as if the thought of children was rather offensive.

"Yes, I told you my grandkids are here for the holidays," Delia said, a bit sharply.

Agatha grunted, clearly displeased. "You can get your blasted hot chocolates later on. It's very important that we all go to Ingrid's house. She has an update for us."

Delia was about to refuse. After all, she hadn't seen her grandchildren for months and she only had them for a week or two. She was enjoying every moment with them now. However, then she felt a tingle in her hand. A small wisp of smoke streamed out, like a ribbon, into the air.

It was true, her powers had been turned up a notch since the solstice, and she felt supercharged.

A small smile tugged at her mouth. The boost to her own magic hadn't troubled her, not nearly as much as it seemed to be bothering Marjie and Agatha at any rate. Perhaps it was because Delia had been working so hard these past few weeks to tame her unruly magic. She'd developed quite a knack for it. It was like a muscle she'd been working to tone and strengthen. Sure, she still had to keep working at it, but it wasn't much of a bother anymore. Although she could hardly practice with the kids around, she and Kitty had been sneaking out to the yard late at night and they'd had a riot setting things on fire. She needed an outlet.

Her growing mastery made Delia feel slightly less of a novice, especially when these far more experienced witches were struggling to contain their newly enhanced elemental magic, but she was prepared to help, all the same.

Still, what to do with the grandkids remained a question.

"Perhaps I could bring the children," Delia suggested.

"This is not a playdate, Delia," Agatha said sternly. "Bring the grandchildren if you must, but we have serious matters to attend to."

"Will it be safe for them?" Delia didn't want to disappoint Merryn and Keyne by leaving them behind. She could give them a bit of a forest walk, let them safely explore around Ingrid's hut while she met with the other crones, and then they could get hot chocolate on the way home.

"Of course, it will be safe," Agatha assured her. "Since we unleashed our powers at the solstice, we've been able to restore the invisibility magic, cloaking the town. You know that. Those fools can't get in. And don't you go running off and breaking it again."

"I won't," Delia said, trying to stop herself from pouting. She was surely far too mature for that kind of carry-on.

"Quite frankly, our powers, as they are, are the most dangerous thing right now. We need to get to that third stage of unlocking them, and for that, we need a plan. Besides, the Sisterhood is up to something!"

"What do you mean?" Delia asked.

Agatha let out a weary groan. "I'm not sure yet, but Ingrid might have an inkling. Her sister is in town."

"Curiouser and curiouser," Delia muttered.

"Exactly, and we need to get the bottom of all of it. Not to mention the grimoires."

"Have you made any progress on yours?" Delia queried.

"No," Agatha admitted, sighing. "But at least I've got mine.

What about you? Have you made any inroads with the Bracewells towards getting your family grimoire?"

"Not really," said Delia. "You don't happen to know them well, do you?"

"Not bloody likely. Why would I go fraternising with snooty toffs like that when I have much more important things to do with my time?" Agatha cackled.

"Fair enough," Delia conceded. "Alright, I'll come along, and I'll probably bring the grandkids with me."

With that, the phone call was ended, and Delia had new plans for the day.

9
MARJIE

Marjie's hands moved gracefully as she prepared another pot of tea, but she couldn't help noticing how the water rippled in response to her gaze, a reminder of how much her powers had grown recently. It wasn't just in manipulating the element of water; she could feel the emotions of every person she met, a tide of feelings that ebbed and flowed around her.

The bell above the door chimed, and Marjie looked up to see a woman with long silver hair in plaits walking in.

Recognition dawned instantly – it was Mathilda, Ingrid's sister, who had helped them evade the Order of Crimson at the farmhouse. It felt like years had passed since then, though it had been barely two weeks.

"Hello, Mathilda," Marjie greeted her warmly, observing

the woman's demeanour. Despite her smile, Mathilda seemed anxious.

Mathilda returned the greeting, her smile not quite reaching her eyes. "Hello, Marjie. It's nice to see you again."

Without asking, Marjie selected a slice of cake for Mathilda, choosing one that she felt would suit her guest's current state of mind. She placed it on a plate, handing it over with a small silver fork. "Take this to a table and I'll bring you some tea. Then we can chat," she said, her tone inviting and gentle.

Mathilda took the plate, her hands trembling ever so slightly. "Thank you, Marjie. I appreciate it."

As Marjie prepared the tea, she observed Mathilda settling at a table, the cake untouched for the moment. Joining her a few minutes later with a pot of freshly brewed tea, Marjie poured two cups and sat down opposite Mathilda.

"So, what brings you to my teashop today?" Marjie asked, her tone friendly but curious.

Mathilda took a deep breath as if gathering her thoughts. "I'm here on behalf of the Sisterhood. We...we want to offer help to you and the other crones."

Marjie raised an eyebrow. "Help? Why now?"

"It's hard to explain," Mathilda began, her voice faltering. "There are things happening, shifts in power. The Sisterhood believes that the Crones are important. We want to support you, protect you from the Order of Crimson."

Marjie took a sip of her tea, considering Mathilda's words. "And why should we trust the Sisterhood? Ingrid..."

Mathilda nodded, her expression earnest. "I understand your hesitation. My sister likes to keep her distance. We're not asking you to join us or change your ways. Just...let us help. There's more at stake than just our individual groups."

Marjie looked at Mathilda, sensing the sincerity in her plea, yet also the undercurrent of fear and uncertainty. "I can't speak for the others, Mathilda. This is something we'll have to discuss together."

Mathilda reached for the slice of cake, her fingers wrapping around the fork. "I understand that. I just hope you'll consider it."

Marjie watched her for a moment, her powers allowing her to feel the turmoil within Mathilda. "We'll consider it," she said finally. "That's all I can promise."

Mathilda nodded, a look of relief crossing her face. "Thank you, Marjie. That's all I can ask for."

"And what about Ingrid? Have you been to see her yet?" Marjie inquired, her tone soft but probing.

Mathilda's gaze dropped to the cake on her plate. "Not yet, I'm on my way there now," she admitted. "You must understand. Ingrid and I...we're not close. Not anymore."

Marjie offered a sad smile, empathising with the complexity of familial relationships. "Ingrid isn't the easiest person in the world, and besides, I know the feeling. I, myself, am long overdue to reconnect with my brother, but I'm trying."

Mathilda smiled sadly. "In that case, I wish you luck."

"Try your cake, dear," Marjie insisted.

Mathilda hesitated for a moment before taking a bite. Hr

eyes widened in surprise and delight. "You are a most powerful witch," she declared, a note of genuine wonder in her voice.

Marjie chuckled softly, her smile warm and knowing. "Thank you, Mathilda. Sometimes, a little sweetness can make difficult paths easier to tread."

10
DELIA

Merryn decisively informed Delia that the hot chocolates had to come first. And so it was that they went for hot chocolates promptly after lunch, enjoying some delightful beverages served by Marjie's warm-hearted friend, Papa Jack, before venturing into the forest. Delia drove up the winding lanes, surrounded by dense woods.

"The trees aren't supposed to be so green at this time of year," Merryn informed her.

"I think you'll find that this forest is an exception," said Delia with a smile. "Have you ever heard of a microclimate?"

"No," said Merryn.

Delia smiled. "Well, we'll look it up online when we get home and learn all about it, shall we?"

"Yes, please," Keyne agreed.

Delia parked next to Agatha's magically souped-up Mini.

"That's a funny car," said Keyne. Although it looked quite ordinary from the outside, the little boy looked at it with wide-eyed curiosity.

"Is it now?" said Delia, wondering, not for the first time, whether that little cherub could see much deeper than the average bear.

"I wonder if it flies," he added.

Delia patted him dotingly on the shoulder. "Maybe we can ask Agatha when we find her. Come on, time for our forest walk."

They ambled along the path, with Torin, the beagle pup, leading the way, the children delighting in the woods with such joyfulness that time passed rather quickly. And before Delia knew it, Ingrid's hut had emerged.

"Does a witch live there?" Merryn asked with a tone of absolute seriousness.

"Well," said Delia, "if a witch does live there, I'm sure she's a very wise witch." She didn't know what words to use for Ingrid that might not scare the children. She wouldn't exactly call her kind or sweet, and sometimes she behaved rather sternly. However, Delia respected the forest witch far too much to mince words.

"Merryn," Delia added, "this is where my friend Ingrid lives. And you'll also see Agatha who called me this morning, and the wonderful Marjie from the tea shop again."

"Ooh, does she have cakes?" Keyne asked.

"I'm not sure," said Delia, "but perhaps it would be better not to expect them, just in case."

He nodded solemnly.

The door flew open just then, but nobody was behind it.

"That is magic," Keyne announced, and he darted right through the open door.

"Is it magic?" Merryn asked, looking at Delia.

"What do you think?" Delia responded.

Merryn looked her in the eye. "I think you know."

These children are remarkable indeed, Delia thought to herself.

The puppy had been sniffing around near one of Ingrid's goats. He gave a happy bark and followed them into the hut.

"Ah, there you all are," Ingrid said to the new arrivals.

Marjie and Agatha were already seated around the table.

"Where's Kitty?" Ingrid asked.

"Back at my house," Delia said. "I didn't know she was invited."

"Neither were the grandchildren," said Agatha, wryly."

"Nonsense. Of course they are!" Ingrid said, smiling.

"Thank you," Merryn said.

"I like to be invited," Keyne added.

"You're welcome, and feel free to roam around the hut," Ingrid replied, then turned to Delia. "Now, take a seat. I have some chamomile tea brewing, and we're going to need it."

Ingrid gracefully carried the teapot to the table, which was a relief. Delia wasn't sure how she would explain her usual floating crockery theatrics to the children. Perhaps Ingrid had more sensitivity than Delia had given her credit for.

"Now, you must tell me, how has everything been going?" Ingrid asked the children, looking quite serious.

"Well, we had Christmas," Merryn said.

"And then we played with our toys," Keyne added. "And Mummy is a bit sick."

Ingrid narrowed her eyes and looked at them both.

"I'm sorry to hear that," said Marjie. "You poor loves."

"It'll be fine. Mummy's very strong," Merryn reassured her.

"Of course she is, and your mother raised strong children too," Marjie added with a smile. She produced some delicious oat and honey biscuits, allowing the children to take two each. Having gobbled their biscuits and sipped their tea, the children busied themselves exploring the hut while the crones spoke in hushed tones.

"Now, what progress have you made on your grimoires?" Ingrid asked, sounding a lot like a school teacher asking about late homework.

"Not much, I'm afraid," Delia admitted. "I met this strange, posh young woman – Elamina Bracewell-Thorn – who came to my door. Apparently she's my cousin. I'll see what else I can find out."

"You be careful around her, dear," said Marjie. "Let me know if you need me to come with you."

"And what about you, Marjie? What progress have you made?" Ingrid asked.

Marjie sighed. "I've been trying to call my brother, but he won't pick up or return my calls, I'm afraid. Even if I do get hold of him, I don't know how he is going to react. It's been so long since we've spoken."

"Well, suck it up," Agatha interjected. "If he doesn't respond well, we'll just have to do a locating spell on your grimoire and steal it."

"Couldn't we try that first?" Marjie asked, but then decided against it. "No, I suppose I'd better at least ask." She sighed and helped herself to some more chamomile tea.

"Our powers are overcharged at the moment," Ingrid said thoughtfully. "We need mastery, and for that, I'm certain we need the grimoires. I'm sure that's the third stage."

"Why do you suppose there are three stages?" Delia asked.

"Good things come in threes," Ingrid responded.

Agatha nodded sternly, confirming that this was a fact and not some kind of foolish superstition, which was how it sounded to Delia.

"Okay then," said Delia. "I have been feeling like my powers have intensified. It used to be that I didn't know how to control them, and I'd set things on fire randomly, but now I can control them reasonably well. It's just that I need to let off steam at night when the kids are asleep."

"Good girl," Marjie said approvingly, somehow managing to sound unpatronising. "I'm glad you're doing that. My main problem is that I keep bursting into tears. Poor Rosemary and Athena don't know what to do with me."

At that moment, as if to demonstrate, a large tear emerged from Marjie's eye and slid down her cheek. She pulled out a handkerchief and patted it away.

"Your empathy is turned up to full volume, I suppose," Delia suggested.

"What about you, Agatha? Have you noticed anything strange?" Marjie asked, wiping away another tear.

"Blasted wind," Agatha grumbled. "It's terrorising me."

"You're terrorising yourself, you mean," Delia pointed out.

Agatha gave her a stern look. "I resent that. It sneaks up on me. I'll be about to enjoy a quiet sherry and a bloody cyclone of books will accost me, so I stand by my original statement. It's terrorising me – and even worse – it's terrorising my library!"

"It's *your* power," Ingrid said, drily. "Perhaps you need to take a leaf out of Delia's book and blow off some steam."

Agatha looked as if she'd bitten into a lemon but said nothing more.

"What about you, Ingrid?" Marjie asked, changing the subject.

"I'm alright during the day, but at night, occasionally, I cause a little earthquake. It seems to be localised to the earth directly under the house, but if this goes on too long, it's only intensifying, which could mean quite dire consequences for us all," Ingrid confessed.

"Why do you think this third stage will help us control our unhinged powers?" Delia asked.

"The book suggests as much." Ingrid waved her hand towards the ancient grimoire.

Just then, the door creaked open, and in walked Mephistos, as smarmy and arrogant as ever. He sniffed the air and, with a disgusted look, said, "Dog! Eugh! How revolting."

"Excuse me," Delia exclaimed, "that's my familiar you're talking about."

Mephistos looked around. "And where is he?"

A faint squeal sounded from outside behind the house.

"The children!" Delia cried.

"They must have gone out the back," Marjie said. "I didn't even notice!"

"Oh no, the dragon!" Ingrid started, but Delia didn't wait to hear more. She was on her feet and out the back door as swiftly as she could possibly move.

The shrieks quickly turned into giggles, and it took a while for Delia to realise that the children were excited not scared.

Before them was a little puppy, just slightly larger than Torin, but adorable.

Delia stared at the puppy. "Where did you come from?"

A green shimmer ran over his fur.

"Ingrid!" Delia said, as the other crones joined her on the back doorstep.

"What is it?" Ingrid asked.

Delia lowered her voice. "Your dragon seems to have transformed himself into a puppy."

"Oh blast it!" said Ingrid. "There goes all my training."

Delia giggled as the children and the two dogs ran around the garden. "Don't tell me you were trying to train your dragon."

"Of course not," said Ingrid. "The dragon was training me, and now we don't have a dragon; we have a puppy. Blast it all!"

Agatha began to chuckle, and Marjie joined her. And before

long, the four Crones were all giggling hysterically on the back doorstep.

"What's so funny?" Mephistos asked from behind them. He took one look at the scene in the back garden with not one but two dogs, turned, and walked out through the front door.

"I hope you didn't have anything important to share with us," said Delia, as the little black tail slunk around the side of the door and out of sight. "Because I don't know if he'll be visiting for a while."

"He's not usually especially useful," said Agatha.

Just then, as the puppy let out a bark that turned into a roar, a few flames burst forth, revealing the dragon's form for a fleeting moment.

The children screamed in delight and excitement.

"Did you see that?" Merryn exclaimed, eyes wide with wonder.

"Yes, I saw it," Delia replied. "This is a strange place, you understand? Perhaps we were just imagining..."

"No," Merryn insisted, her conviction unwavering. "It was real."

Marjie caught her eye, sharing a conspiratorial grin, and gave her a knowing wink.

II
THE SHEPHERD

Father Benedict paced back and forth in his new tower room like a caged predator. The space was opulent and imposing, with tall, narrow windows that offered a panoramic view of the Order's grounds. Some things remained the same. He was among familiar items – the heavy oak desk, laden with scrolls and artifacts of power, which sat under a large, intricately detailed tapestry depicting the Order's victories throughout the ages.

The recent betrayal by the Cleric, his once most trusted, if somewhat inept, disciple, played over in his mind.

Benedict had always known the man was not his intellectual equal, but his loyalty had seemed unwavering.

The sting of betrayal was sharp, yet Father Benedict couldn't help but acknowledge a grudging respect for the Cleric's unexpected audacity.

In a twisted way, the situation had presented him with the perfect opportunity – a chance to assert his supremacy – but only if he played his cards right.

He paused his pacing and stood by the window, his hands clasped behind his back as he gazed out at the sprawling compound below.

Contributing to the Order had been his life's work, his divine calling, always with the Almighty's will as his compass. But now, he saw a new path unfolding before him – one that required him to seize absolute control.

The Elders, wise and venerable as they were, had become complacent in their authority, letting the compound fall into slovenly disarray. They failed to see the shifting tides, the new challenges that the modern world presented.

Besides, Father Benedict had always harboured a vision of the Order's destiny that far exceeded the narrow scope of the Elders' understanding. It was time for a new era under his leadership.

His gaze drifted to the ancient tome on his desk, its pages filled with forgotten knowledge and prophecies. He had spent countless hours poring over its contents, seeking guidance and insight. The tome had never steered him wrong. It spoke of change, of a great upheaval that would elevate the Order to unprecedented heights.

Father Benedict turned from the window and strode to his desk, his mind alight with possibilities. The Cleric's betrayal, though painful, was merely a stepping stone to greater things.

It was the catalyst he needed to cast aside the shackles of the Elders' outdated governance.

He would need to be cautious, of course. The Elders were not fools, and they would not relinquish their authority without a fight. But Father Benedict had always been a master of manipulation and strategy. He knew the inner workings of the Order like the back of his hand, and he was confident in his ability to outmanoeuvre any opposition.

A cold smile touched his lips as he sat down at his desk, his fingers tracing the ancient symbols carved into its surface. The future of the Order was in his hands, and he would shape it according to his vision. The Almighty had chosen him for this moment, and he would not fail.

The Cleric's fate was a cautionary tale – a reminder of what happened to those who dared to challenge Father Benedict's authority. But it was also a stepping stone, a necessary sacrifice on the path to glory. The Order of Crimson would rise to new heights under his leadership, and nothing would stand in his way.

12

DELIA

As the grandchildren danced away through the forest, with Marjie, Agatha, and the puppy following close behind, Delia felt a hand on her shoulder and jumped.

"Ah, sorry, dear," said Marjie. "I didn't mean to startle you."

"What is it?" Delia asked, turning towards her friend.

Marjie sighed. "Since you and I are the only two Crones not to have our grimoires, I was wondering whether you'd mind buddying up."

"You're going to need all the help you can get," said Agatha.

"That sounds good to me," Delia agreed. "What do you have in mind?"

"Well, if my brother will ever agree to meet with me, I'd really appreciate the moral support. I'd bring Rosemary, but she doesn't know about our secrets…"

"Of course," said Delia. "Doesn't he live in Yorkshire or

something? We could make a trip of it and stay somewhere nice."

Tears welled in Marjie's eyes. She quickly wiped them away with a sniffle, her voice choked with emotion. "Thank you, love. I really appreciate it."

"No trouble at all," said Delia, keen to have something to keep her on her toes. "And does that mean you'll help me with the Bracewells?"

"Of course," Marjie said resolutely. "I don't mind giving them a piece of my mind. It's probably been a long time coming, after how that family treated my poor mother."

Delia smiled sympathetically. "Let's hope it doesn't come to that. I was thinking I might just try to call Elamina, have a chat, get to know her a bit better. Maybe they'll invite me to their house. I'm assuming they have a very fancy house."

"Indeed they do," said Marjie. "They're too snobby to be in Myrtlewood, so it's slightly further afield. Rosemary says it's a grand mansion."

"I'm sure it is," said Delia. "I know hoity-toity people when I see them; I've spent years in high-end theatre, remember?"

"Of course," said Marjie, with a grin.

"Nana, hurry up!" Merryn called.

Delia chuckled and began walking a little faster through the forest.

Again, she had that feeling as if somebody was watching. She looked through the trees; there was nobody in sight.

"What is it, dear?" Marjie asked.

"Just spooked," said Delia.

Agatha cackled. "What kind of witch are you if you don't feel like you're the scariest thing out here?"

Delia glared at her. "I think we'd all agree that you are the scariest thing out here, Agatha."

"I'm not joking," Agatha said sternly, while Delia and Marjie laughed like schoolchildren.

"I bet you can't wait to get home to your magical sherry decanter," said Marjie. "So let's get a move on. And as for those Bracewells," she added to Delia, "you wouldn't exactly be stealing if you took their Grimoire, by the way."

"Wouldn't I?" Delia raised an eyebrow.

"Marjie's right, it's your family Grimoire too," said Agatha. "Always remember that. And family grimoires can't really be stolen by members of the family. In fact, is it really stealing at all if it's from family?"

"I'm not sure how much of a family member they consider me to be," Delia mused. "I got the impression that Elamina was only checking up on me to see if I was after money, which I am certainly not. I don't want to give them the impression that I want anything from them, even though technically I do. I need that book."

"It's wise not to show your hand," said Agatha. "I'll give you credit for that."

Delia smiled. "Why thank you, Agatha, that almost sounded like a compliment."

"In your wildest dreams," Agatha said with an ironic air, "but do be wary around those Bracewells. They might be brusque and clad in fine silks, but they are wily in their own way and dreadfully dangerous."

Marjie gulped. "Agatha is right; they've done all sorts of nefarious things. And the last thing we need is for you to get caught up in it."

"Maybe I should come with you to see them," said Agatha, to which Marjie and Delia exchanged a look.

"I'm not sure if that would be the most diplomatic and tactful approach," Delia replied.

Agatha chortled. "I'm not sure whether to take that as an insult or a compliment. So I'll just do both simultaneously."

13

INGRID

Ingrid took a moment to relax into the quietude of her hut, contemplating her new-found friends. Marjie was always so full of fire and determination, Ingrid mused, a faint smile gracing her lips.

Her spirit is as unyielding as an ancient oak. Yet, beneath that fierce exterior lies a heart that cares deeply for us all.

She admired Marjie's blend of strength and compassion, a rare combination that made her an invaluable member of their circle.

Her mind then shifted to Agatha, with her sharp mind and sharper tongue. She knew all too well how Agatha's grumpy exterior could be misleading.

Her unwavering rationality has been our anchor, even if her methods can be...unorthodox.

Ingrid chuckled softly as she put away the tea things with a quick flourish of magic and made her way to the back garden to check on the dragon.

As she stepped outside, her gaze fell upon the place where Delia had stood moments before. *Dear Delia, still finding her way...There's so much potential in her, like a seed waiting to sprout.*

The dragon was there, still obstinately masquerading as a puppy. Ingrid found her sleeping next to the ancient elder tree, bathed in its magic. Finally, her thoughts turned inward as she gazed at the quiet garden, bathed in twilight.

And what of me? The one who listens, who watches.

A soft sigh escaped her lips.

The dragon puppy opened her ancient eyes and yawned.

The garden was alive with the scents and sounds of the encroaching night. Ingrid's senses, so finely attuned to the natural world, picked up the gentle rustle of leaves and the distant hoot of an owl. Her eyes scanned the scene before her. The dragon-puppy got up and rushed towards her shimmering faintly in the low light, before rushing away, playfully, towards the bed of artemisia.

"Frolicking?"

Ingrid didn't know whether to feel frustration or amusement. She knew the dragon was far more than she appeared – a being of ancient magic and untold power, yet here she was, playing in the garden with the carefree abandon of a young animal.

She reached out with her mind, trying to communicate with the dragon. The connection was elusive, like trying to grasp a wisp of smoke.

She received fleeting impressions – feelings, sensations, and the occasional blurry image that slipped away before she could fully comprehend it. Ingrid's heart raced with the effort, her brow furrowed in concentration, trying to forge a mental link.

Momentarily, her focus wavered. An unbidden memory surfaced, as clear and sudden as a splash of cold water: the sensation of soft fabric beneath her fingertips, the delicate weave of a skirt she once knew. A hand – warm and reassuring – brushed against hers, evoking a sense of longing and lost time.

Then came the sound, a musical laugh that had once filled her days with joy. It was Gwyneth's laugh, a sound as familiar to her as her own heartbeat, yet one she hadn't heard in countless years. The memory was so vivid, so real, that Ingrid was transported back to those long-lost days.

"Oh, Gwynneth, why must you haunt me now after all these years?" she muttered to herself, a note of melancholy in her voice.

It was a whisper to the night, a private acknowledgement of a ghost from her past. The memory was gentle, yet it carried the sting of old wounds.

Ingrid shook her head, as if to physically dispel the past. She refocused her attention on the dragon-puppy, pushing the lingering traces of sorrow to the back of her mind.

Now was not the time for dwelling on the past; she had a present mystery to unravel. The cool night air and the subtle scent of wormwood helped to anchor her back in the moment, back to the task at hand.

With a deep breath, Ingrid re-centred herself, her gaze once again meeting the dragon's playful, wise eyes as she approached. Ingrid reached out, placing a hand respectfully on the dragon's soft puppy head. She was here, now, with this enigmatic creature, and that was what mattered.

A clearer image emerged: a cloud. Ingrid paused, puzzled by the simplicity and seeming randomness of this vision. A cloud – so ordinary and yet, coming from the dragon, it must hold some significance.

Ingrid reflected on the nature of clouds – ever-changing, transient, and yet part of something much larger, the endless cycle of water and air. Was the dragon trying to convey something about change, about the impermanence and interconnectedness of all things? Or was it a more literal message, something imminent in the skies?

Settling herself beside the playful dragon-puppy, Ingrid spoke softly, her voice tinged with both affection and exasperation. "I know there's more to you than these puppy antics. You're an ancient being, aren't you? What are you trying to tell me with these games?"

The dragon-puppy cocked its head, its eyes glinting with an intelligence that belied its form. It let out a soft whine, almost as if understanding her words, yet unable to respond in kind.

"I've lived long enough to know that appearances can be deceiving. You, in this form, are a perfect example. But why a cloud? What are you trying to tell me?"

The puppy wagged its tail, then paused, looking up at the sky. Ingrid followed its gaze, observing the night sky where clouds drifted lazily. "Is it about change? The impermanence of things?"

The dragon-puppy yawned, then nuzzled closer to Ingrid, her warmth comforting against the chill of the night. Ingrid smiled down, her frustration softening. "You're quite the enigma, aren't you? A powerful creature of ancient legend, choosing to be a small, earthbound being. There's a lesson in humility in there somewhere for me, I suppose."

The dragon looked up at Ingrid with eyes that seemed to hold the wisdom of the ages, then playfully nipped at her hand. "Or maybe you're just reminding me to not take everything so seriously."

As she sat there, the old memory re-surfaced, but the scent of damp earth and pine needles brought Ingrid back to the present. She looked at the puppy-dragon, now sitting quietly, its eyes holding a depth that betrayed its true nature.

The dragon had, indeed, been training her, and this playful guise was clearly also a lesson – a reminder of the importance of perspective, of seeing beyond the obvious, of appreciating the magic in play and the mystique of the unexpected.

14
DELIA

The pub was bustling, but Marjie and Agatha managed to secure a table for the group without much effort at all, as several people who had just finished their meals got up to make room.

"You two are celebrities, aren't you?" said Delia. "After everything I heard about the winter solstice and what went down at Thorn Manor, I'm not surprised."

"It was nothing, dear," said Marjie.

"Maybe not for you," said Agatha, "I had a hell of a time trying to get people in line. It's like herding cats, I tell you."

Merryn and Keyne were thrilled to be out and about in Myrtlewood. They stared at all the unusual townsfolk in the pub, many dressed in capes and cloaks and brightly coloured clothing of purple and green.

"This place is magical," Merryn said decisively.

Kitty winked at her and nudged Delia.

Liam arrived at the table to take their order and Delia tried not to blush. Her last interaction with her sort-of-landlord had been a bit awkward.

"Ah, Delia, Marjie, Agatha, and these must be the grand-children." Liam beamed and Delia introduced them.

"And who's your new friend?" Liam asked.

"Kitty, darling." Kitty batted her eyelashes at him.

Delia rolled her eyes. "Seriously?"

"What will you be having this evening?" Liam asked, mentioning he was helping Sherry out since it was a busy night.

"Such a good boy," Marjie said, patting him affectionately on the arm.

The children excitedly ordered fish and chips. Delia settled for a hearty stew, as did the other crones, whereas Kitty opted for a steak.

"They should call this the Crone's stew," said Delia after they all placed their orders.

"Now I feel left out," said Kitty. "What do I have to do to get into your club?"

"It's not a club," said Delia.

"You're not even supposed to know about it, really," said Agatha. "So perhaps keep your mouth shut."

"Oh, she's a grumpy old bat, isn't she?" Kitty said with a laugh.

Agatha glared at her.

"Come on, cut her some slack," Delia implored Agatha.

"Kitty's very new to all this. I'm not saying she's not always badly behaved, because, quite frankly, that's one of the things I love about her. But at least give her a few weeks to settle in before you get annoyed with her."

Agatha sighed. "Should have ordered a second sherry," she said, taking a rather large gulp and emptying her glass. "I'll be right back," she announced, making her way to the bar.

"I like her," said Kitty. "Good, stroppy old woman."

"Don't worry, there's plenty of those around here..." said Delia. She glanced across the room, and her blood ran cold.

It wasn't a red cloak, it was a dark brown one, partially obscuring a very familiar face.

She recognised him immediately, despite the lack of his hat.

"Excuse me a moment," she said to Marjie and Kitty before lowering her voice. "Keep the children safe. Whatever you do, don't take your eyes off them."

Delia stood up and stormed over to the table.

"What are you doing here?" she asked, her voice trembling.

Declan raised his hood just slightly, his grey eyes taking her in. "Having dinner," he said, gesturing to the bowl of stew in front of him.

"How dare you come in here after everything you've—" Delia's voice faltered.

"What have I done exactly?" Declan said, the corner of his mouth twitching in an infuriating way.

"You know—" said Delia, and then she stopped. What had Declan done? He'd stalked her – that was bad enough – and worked with the Order; that alone was a horrendous thing.

"You know exactly what you've done." She glared daggers at him. He returned her gaze unfazed.

Delia felt her breath quicken, and she took a step back.

"Delia..." he said.

She felt a tugging sensation in her chest that only fuelled her burning rage.

He put his spoon down on the table. "You have no idea of the terrible things I've done over the years, over the centuries. This..." He gestured around. "This was nothing."

His dismissiveness was shocking.

"How can you say that?" she asked, taking care to hold in her magic to as not to incinerate everything in sight. "You put me, my friends, my family at risk with your actions. How can you say that's nothing? How heartless of you."

Only then did he break eye contact, looking down at the table and pushing away his bowl of stew. "I've been heartless for a long time," he growled.

"Leave here, now!" said Delia.

He looked back up at her.

"I can't," Declan replied.

Delia grasped her own palms at hot steam emerged from them. "Don't be ridiculous, of course you can. You've caused enough trouble..."

"I was just doing my job," he replied.

Delia scowled. "Many evils in this world have been committed by people who were just doing their job," she retorted, glimpsing a fire burning in his eyes. Perhaps it was rage, or something else.

"Back off," Delia said. "Get away from here and leave me alone."

Declan did not at all seem afraid for his life. He was oddly silent, like the eye in the middle of the storm.

"It's admirable that you protect the ones you love," he remarked, looking over to her grandchildren.

Delia burned with fury over the passive-aggressive threat. She was about to scorch him into oblivion when she felt a hand on her arm; Marjie and Agatha had arrived at her side.

"What's going on? Who's this?" asked Agatha.

"It's that man," said Marjie. "He was following us, working with the Order."

"The Order can't be in here," Agatha grumbled.

"Is this man bothering you?" asked Liam, arriving at the table.

"Just enjoying a quiet meal," Declan replied.

"What's going on?" It was Covvey, appearing now beside them. "If she says he's bothering her, he's bothering her. Get him out of here," he growled.

Delia took a step back, her rage dissipating in the chaos.

She glanced back over to the table to see Kitty and the children still safely in place, though Kitty was shooting her furtive glances.

Covvey was now leaning menacingly towards Declan, and Delia no longer knew what to make of the situation.

Declan was not what she expected. She could not sense any malice in him at all. Besides, he hadn't given the crones away to the Order when they escaped the abandoned hamlet. Had he tried to protect her from going into the theatre? Or had that been another of the Order's tricks to throw her off her game? She was so sick and tired of people messing with her mind!

As her rage blazed again, she had a right mind to set the man on fire, but before she could manage it, there was a puff of black smoke, a glimmer of what could have been the edge of a portal. He disappeared.

"I showed him, I did," said Covvey. "Never you mind, Delia. I'll keep you safe."

"You don't need to come in here all threatening," said Liam. "I was sorting it out."

"You're just a lad," said Covvey, though Liam was clearly a full-grown man. "What would you know?" They glared at each other.

Delia sighed and shrugged, looking from Marjie to Agatha.

Marjie's smile was warm, but Agatha looked grumpier than ever. "Look, the food's arrived, and it'll be getting cold," she said.

"He's an enigma, that man," said Marjie, as Agatha shuffled away.

They made their way back to the table.

Merryn and Keyne looking at her with startled curiosity.

"Who was that man, Nana?" Merryn asked.

Keyne looked interested. "Is he a bad man?"

"He's no one important," Delia replied.

"But you were so angry," Keyne said.

"He's not supposed to be here, that's all," Marjie interjected.

"Why not?" Merryn asked.

"He's banned," Agatha said sternly. "He's not supposed to be in this town at all."

"I didn't know you could be banned from a town," Merryn said.

"I hope I'm not banned," Keyne added thoughtfully.

"Of course, you're not." Delia affectionately patted his shoulder.

Keyne smiled at her.

Just then, there was a loud throat-clearing sound. Delia turned to see none other than Ferg, the mayor of Myrtlewood, standing next to her. He wasn't a tall man, yet he was somehow quite gangly, with lanky limbs protruding from a bright purple cloak.

"Can I help you?" Delia asked.

Ferg gave her a serious look. "I sincerely hope you're not causing more trouble."

"Trouble? Me?" Delia replied.

Agatha laughed. "She's always trouble."

Marjie shot her a quelling look.

Ferg crossed his arms and straightened his spine. "I've heard stories. You three have been up to no good." He gestured to the Crones.

"And who's this?" His eyes landed on Kitty, who extended her hand to him.

"I'm Kitty," she introduced herself.

He took her hand with ceremonial grace. "A pleasure to

meet you. I'm Ferg, the mayor of this fine town. You are most welcome to stay, but do be careful who you associate with."

Kitty hooted with laughter.

"I certainly hope that none of you are causing trouble," Ferg continued. "Especially you newcomers to the town. I'm carefully monitoring you."

"Monitoring?" Merryn asked. "Do you have an ankle bracelet like the criminals in Mummy's court cases, Nana?"

"No, that would be ridiculous," Delia said.

"How are they monitoring you?" Keyne asked.

"The mayor here is apparently just making sure that I'm not causing trouble, which I am certainly not," Delia replied calmly.

"Glad to hear it," said Ferg. "And now that you're settled in the village, I would like to once again extend my invitation for you to take up the position of director in our local Myrtlewood Players theatre troupe."

Delia took deep, slow breaths and exhaled, summoning her wit. She needed to tactfully decline the mayor's offer without being rude and risk being labelled as even more of a troublemaker.

"That sounds like so much fun, Nana!" Merryn said.

"Oh yes, can we come too?" Keyne added.

"You most certainly can," Ferg said, before Delia had a chance to protest. "In fact, we have a rehearsal tomorrow. I'll expect to see you there at noon in the town hall."

Delia cleared her throat, but the looks of absolute joy on the children's faces stopped her in her tracks. Sensing her moment of weakness, Ferg decided to take his leave without giving her a chance to back out of the situation.

"I can't wait," Keyne said. "It will be so much fun."

Delia sighed, exchanging pitiful glances with Kitty before pulling her lips up into a smile.

"Suppose it could be a bit of fun," she said. The smiles on her grandchildren's faces made it almost worthwhile – almost.

Delia ate her meal in relative silence, or as much silence as could be had with two children, a sassy best friend, and two crones.

Delia couldn't help but glance back in the direction of where Declan had been. What was he playing at? Whatever it was, this game made her dreadfully uncomfortable.

15
AGATHA

Agatha cautiously pushed the door ajar to her sanctuary, the library. Its towering shelves and ancient wisdom awaited her, a bastion against the day's disquiet. It was blessedly still.

She took a deep breath, closing the door behind her with a soft click. She needed this solace now, more than she usually did, for the evening at the pub had stirred unwelcome emotions. Yet, as she crossed the threshold, her inner turmoil seemed to seep into the very walls of the room, the air growing more restless with every step.

The books, her silent, steadfast companions, began to tremble on their shelves.

"Oh blast it all. Not again!"

She was out of control of her own mind again, lost in a tumult of inner conflict. She recalled the scene at the pub –

Covvey, with that instinctive, protective lunge towards Delia. The image burned behind her eyes, and as the volumes on the shelves rocked more violently on their shelves, the papers on her desk took flight.

Agatha tried to suppress her thoughts, to calm herself, but they betrayed her. Another surge of papers spiralled upward. Books flew from their resting places like startled birds.

"Calm yourselves!" she commanded, her voice quivering, but the volumes only spun faster, mirroring the spiralling of her thoughts.

Covvey rushing forward, shielding Delia, and Agatha, watching, sidelined, her hands balled into fists at her sides. The protective gesture felt like a personal affront, an illogical sense of betrayal that she could neither justify nor dismiss.

She reached out to still a passing tome, but it jerked away, and she withdrew her hand as if burned.

She was angry at everyone, yet she knew Covvey hadn't done anything wrong. It was simply that he was Agatha's friend and a part of her didn't want him falling for anyone in case it got in the way. She scolded herself for harbouring such irrational feelings.

Agatha Twigg, historian, scholar, and mistress of the logical, was at the mercy of the very thing she had always held at arm's length – the raw, uncharted territory of her emotions.

As Agatha braced herself against the howling winds that ripped through her library, her thoughts whirled back to countless evenings at the pub with Covvey.

Side by side at their usual table, they had shared more than just ale; they had exchanged fragments of their lives. Covvey, with his quiet strength and wry humour, had been a constant in her life, a comrade in arms in the often solitary pursuit of knowledge.

Their camaraderie had been a comforting beacon, illuminating even the darkest corners of her scholarly pursuits. Even though she'd never possessed romantic qualities herself, she hated the thought of losing a cherished confidant to someone else.

Standing firm against the gale, Agatha closed her eyes, seeking the eye of the storm within herself.

She drew in a deep breath, the air mixed with the dust of disturbed tomes and the scent of ancient ink. She reached for the calm centre of her vast knowledge, the part of her that understood the laws of nature and magic alike.

Resistance had only fed the chaos. Now, she sought a different path – acceptance.

Within the dark sanctuary of her mind, she addressed the unwelcome feelings. She might not like them, but they were a part of her as much as her intellect. She grudgingly accepted their existence, allowed them space within her. The tension in her shoulders eased, her fists unclenched, and she exhaled a breath that she had been holding within the confines of her rigid control.

As she did so, the wild storm of the library began to slow. The papers started to drift down like leaves in a gentle breeze, the books' fluttering pages coming to rest. The air settled, and the quiet that followed was not the oppressive silence of before but a peaceful hush, the kind that falls after rain.

Agatha opened her eyes to a scene of utter disarray, but there was a new lightness to her being.

The storm had passed and now she had to reorder her beloved library.

Agatha extended her arms, her fingers dancing in the air as she began to recite one of her favourite incantations.

The words, familiar and potent, flowed from her lips with firmness and calm, each syllable infused with the power of her will and the newfound acceptance of her heart.

As the enchantment wove through the library, a quiet magic took hold.

One by one, books levitated from the floor, their covers flapping like the wings of homing birds as they soared gracefully to their shelves. They slipped into their designated spaces with a satisfying soft thud, the spine of each volume aligning perfectly with its neighbours.

Papers lying scattered on the floor, now glided through the air with an elegant choreography. They spun and settled into neat stacks upon her desk, arranging themselves with an almost sentient precision.

The furniture shifted back into place. The legs of chairs and tables found their familiar grooves in the carpet.

Even the dust picked itself up and drifted towards the nearby bin, disappearing from sight, leaving every surface pristine and aglow in the lamplight.

Agatha watched, a gentle smile curving her lips as the last of the disorder rectified itself before her eyes, every piece returned to its rightful place, every element obedient to her command.

As the last book nestled into its nook, the library stood once more as a room of tranquillity and refuge. The room was still, and all that remained was the soft whisper of her own breath and the warmth of satisfaction.

But something was out of place, a solitary anomaly that drew Agatha's attention. The family grimoire lay open on her desk as if waiting for her.

She knew she'd put it away the night before, but now it lay waiting for her.

The book was open to 'Elders Blaze,' an old folk poem written in an older style of language that Agatha, with her historian's brain, dated to be late-Middle English – a script easier to understand when read aloud, so she recited the poem, hoping it would reveal something new.

Whenne elders blaze, the soth shal rise,
   In starlit e'en and moonlit skies.
   Their words as sparks of ancient fire,
   Foretelling what shal come to tyre.
   In eche a crease upon their brow,
   A prophecy of then and now.
   They speake of light and dark's amends,
   Where fractured paths to wholeness bends.

. . .

Yon tales of yore, so rich and deep,
 In whispers through the ages creep.
 Of times when light and shadow meet,
 In dance where both shall find their seat.
 Their voices, like a sacred chime,
 Echo forth through passing time.
 Foreseeing when the schism heals,
 And truth to all, it so reveals.

So harken to the elders' call,
 In their wisdom, find thy thrall.
 For when they blaze, so bright and bold,
 A tale of harmony is told.

She'd read this poem before, many times, but now lines that once spoke of history now hinted at secrets and riddles, leaving a furrow of confusion upon her brow.

As Agatha leaned over the tome, retracing the familiar verses with a tentative finger, the pages began to turn of their own volition.

They fluttered with purpose, stopping on a section of her grimoire that she hadn't seen before. The words spoke of a realm so fantastical, it defied reason. A land of cloud? Perhaps it was a metaphor. Agatha was not especially fond of metaphors, finding them infuriatingly inaccurate. She chose instead, to interpret it as a riddle. Agatha was rather fond of riddles.

Her gaze drifted to the fireplace, where the glow of embers cast a warm, inviting light. There, the sherry decanter glinted, its contents untouched by the storm. It called to her, offering solace from the burgeoning sense of wonder that threatened to unsettle her.

16

DELIA

After enjoying a breakfast of pikelets – one of Kitty's specialities – the children spent several hours playing in the garden. Their excitement about the prospect of going to the theatre troupe meeting was obvious.

"It's just a small group," Delia had said, trying to manage their expectations. She didn't want to add that the performances weren't very good, recalling her cringe-worthy experience with the Myrtlewood Players at the winter solstice. Of course, that was only her perspective – and someone with so much experience as herself had a certain sensitivity that the children likely hadn't developed yet. Despite her hesitations, she couldn't help but enjoy their enthusiasm.

"I wonder if I could be in a play," said Merryn dreamily as she put her coat on.

"Of course you can, darling," replied Kitty. "You'd be a star."

"I'm not sure if they're doing any plays while you're around," said Delia. "But maybe we could put on something just for fun and you can join today."

Delia wondered what she was getting herself into as both children began play-acting as characters from Peter Pan. Merryn wanted to be Peter, and Keyne insisted on being Tinkerbell, believing a fairy possessed more powers.

"Fair enough," Kitty said with a smile. "I always fancied being Tinkerbell, or perhaps Peter."

Kitty had been in a rather flat mood that morning. "I just don't know what I'm doing here," she confessed to Delia as they washed the post-breakfast dishes. "I miss my ridiculous boyfriend, although I was getting rather tired of him. And I miss London. This place is quaint and pretty, but there's not much action, really."

"I'm not sure if I need more action after the winter solstice," Delia mused. "A holiday is just what we need. Once we've dealt with the imminent threats, maybe you can return, or we could figure out how to cast a protection spell specifically for you – to keep those horrible men away."

"I appreciate your protectiveness," Kitty said, "but really, those fools are no big threat."

"They kidnapped you," said Delia sternly.

"Only for a little while. It could have been a lot more fun, really."

"You're impossible!" Delia flicked the tea-towel at her and laughed.

No sooner had they finished the dishes than Merryn and Keyne burst into the house asking for lunch.

"How about we go to Marjie's teashop again?" suggested Delia.

"Oh yes, please!" exclaimed Keyne. "I want jam scones."

"Me too," agreed Merryn. "And a pasty?"

Delia smiled. "Alright, jam scones and pasty it is. Let's go."

"The seasons are certainly strange here," Kitty remarked as they made their way into the village, the children running ahead and out of earshot. "I'm sure it was the middle of summer just a few days ago."

"Just be glad we missed all the action," Delia replied. "I hear Marjie and Agatha had a hectic time at the Thorn residence trying to get the seasons back in order."

"I'm surprised you didn't want to go and help your new friends," Kitty said.

Delia sighed. "I was recovering from my own adventure, remember. Besides, they were trying to bring back winter – my fire powers could have gotten in the way."

At the tea shop, they found Marjie looking rather flustered.

"What is it, Marjie?" Delia asked as she, the children, and Kitty settled at a table.

"I still haven't heard back from my brother. I suppose he really doesn't want to see me," Marjie said.

"Maybe he is just busy. It's a funny time of year, you know," Delia suggested.

"I suppose," said Marjie, though she seemed on the verge of tears.

"I can keep trying...it just feels like—"

"It feels like a rejection, doesn't it?"

Marjie nodded and tears welled up in her eyes." Delia gave her a hug to console her. "I can relate. When Gillian didn't want to see me, I felt I'd failed as a parent – or even as a human being. But things are alright now, and I'm sure your brother will come around."

"I wish there was some kind of magic for that." Marjie chuckled sadly. "But it wouldn't be very ethical, would it?"

"Of course not," Delia agreed. "I can't stop thinking about that time years ago when I tripped in the theatre. Jerry engineered that whole situation...I could have gotten up. I keep thinking about it. I could have gotten up and kept going, but I just could not bring myself to. I wonder if it was some sort of magic that held me down. I just couldn't bring myself to...Did he enchant me? Do something to my brain? I can't figure out what made that potentially small failure into such a catastrophe."

"I wouldn't put it past him," said Kitty, who had approached the counter. "That man is bad news. I always knew it."

"It's true, you never liked him," Delia said.

Marjie smiled sadly. "Sometimes our friends' instincts are worth trusting."

"Well, with Kitty, you never know," Delia said, half-jokingly.

"I fancy a chocolate torte," said Kitty. "What does that say about my instincts now?"

"Maybe have a sandwich first or something?" Delia suggested.

"If I'm going to eat more carbs, I want chocolate," Kitty insisted, crossing her arms.

Delia laughed. "Fine then. You're an adult. You're most welcome to have chocolate for lunch."

Marjie chuckled. "I'll bring it right over, dear."

17
MARJIE

Marjie released a satisfied sigh as she poured hot water over loose tea leaves with a practiced hand, her movements deliberate and gentle. Delia, Kitty, and the children had just left the teashop, leaving the space calm and relatively quiet as few customers remained.

Marjie had been practicing pouring the tea for the past few days, finally achieving the delicate balance needed to control her newly potent water magic during such a simple act. The subtle steam rose slowly in spirals, adding to her sense of peace.

The bell above the door chimed. She didn't need to look up to know it was Papa Jack; his presence was as comforting and familiar as the scent of chamomile on a restless night.

"Good afternoon, Marjie," Papa Jack said, his voice a warm rumble.

Marjie smiled, turning to face her good friend. "Afternoon, Papa Jack. The usual, I presume?" she asked, already reaching for the special blend she kept just for him.

"You know me too well." He chuckled, settling into his favourite chair by the window. "How's the day treating you?"

The fine porcelain clinked softly as Marjie set a sunny yellow cup and saucer on the counter. "Oh, you know, the usual ebb and flow," she replied, allowing a small quip at her own expense. "But no tea disasters today, thankfully. I think I might have re-mastered the subtle art of tea making after all!"

Papa Jack's eyes twinkled with mirth. "Glad to hear it. Wouldn't want to be caught in a deluge of Darjeeling." His deep laugh filled the room.

Marjie laughed along with him. "And how are you? How is little Zola?"

"Growing like a weed," he said with a shake of his head. "And just as wild. She keeps me on my toes, like any good grandkid."

Marjie poured the brewed tea into Papa Jack's cup, her magic carefully in check. "That's children for you. They're the very storms we never knew we needed."

Papa Jack accepted the cup with a nod of thanks. "True words, my dear. And speaking of storms, you still haven't told me about the ruckus at the solstice festival. Everything alright?"

Marjie leaned on the counter, her gaze momentarily distant. "Yes, all's well now. It was quite the palaver, but we managed, as we always do."

"Strong as the tide, you lot are," Papa Jack said, taking a sip of his tea. "I always say, there's no messing with the women of Myrtlewood."

"Never a truer word spoken," Marjie agreed, her heart warmed by his words.

As Papa Jack savoured his tea, Marjie busied herself with tidying up the counter. The clink of cutlery and the rush of running water soothed her as usual, as did the quiet presence of her good friend, but her heart ached at all she could not share with him.

Marjie felt the familiar tug at the edge of her mind, the unspoken truths and half-shared tales that lingered between her and Papa Jack. He was one of her dearest friends, yet there were parts of her life, especially now with the Crones, that she had to keep secret. It didn't feel right.

Papa Jack sensed her concern. "You've got that look again, Marjie," he said softly, setting down his cup. "The one that says your mind's crossing troubled waters."

Marjie offered a wry smile. "Just the usual," she assured him, though her heart quickened at the half-truth. Sure enough, magical chaos was now 'the usual' in Myrtlewood, but there was so much she had to hold back.

He smiled warmly. "If you ever do want to share anything, you know I'm here."

"I know, and I'm grateful for it," Marjie said, finding solace in his steadfast presence. She redirected the conversation to safer shores. "I've been thinking of trying to reach out to my brother again."

His eyebrows lifted. "That's a big bridge to build. He still not answering your calls?"

Marjie shook her head, her fingers tracing the rim of a teacup. "No, and I don't expect he will any time soon..."

Papa Jack sighed, rising from his chair to wrap Marjie in a warm hug. "These things take time," he said gently. And Marjie only hoped that he was right.

18

DELIA

Delia's spine stiffened as they approached the town hall. "You don't *have* to do this, you know," Kitty said gently. "Make up an excuse!"

The children were a few paces ahead, balancing on a low wall with their arms outstretched. Delia shot them a look of adoration. "I can't back out now, I have to do it for them."

"What about you?" Kitty asked.

Delia sighed. "Everything about theatre feels tainted now, after the situation with Jerry and finding out all that...my whole life is a lie."

"Don't be ridiculous," Kitty chided. "I knew you before you met that horrible man. You loved theatre long before he came into your life. In fact, he's the one who pushed you into directing and discouraged you from being an actor. You could have taken on the world, been in the limelight instead of backstage."

"Don't be silly," Delia sighed, dismissing the thought. "I'm not getting back on stage."

"You were a star, and I think that horrible experience just made you feel safer pulling strings behind the curtain," Kitty insisted.

Delia shrugged. "Before I knew what Jerry had done, Ferg suggested I get involved in the local theatre, right when I first arrived in Myrtlewood. I thought it was beneath me, I really did....and in some ways, I probably still do. But I didn't realise I'd be scared of it – something so small as this! And now I sound like a snob."

"Of course you are, love," said Kitty. "You just have taste!"

Delia laughed. "I might have taste, but I don't have to be rude about it."

"Speak for yourself," Kitty joked, taking Delia's arm. "Come on, let's just check it out. We don't have to stay long."

They pushed open the town hall doors. Merryn and Keyne ran in ahead, joining the small number of people already assembled, including none other than the extravagant mayor, Ferg.

"Ah! Here she is, the woman of the hour!" Ferg exclaimed. "Ready to take your rightful place as our director?"

Delia gave him a stern look. "Excuse me, your 'magnificent excellency' or whatever it is..."

Ferg's brows furrowed.

"I said I'd come and check it out," Delia reminded him. "I haven't signed up for anything."

"But we need you," Ferg implored. "I can no longer direct, but I'd like to stay in the troupe."

"Really?" Delia raised an eyebrow. "And you don't mind being told what to do by me?"

"If it's for the highest good," Ferg said, bowing elaborately, causing the children to giggle.

"All I'm saying is that I haven't committed to anything. I'm just visiting," Delia clarified.

"What are we going to do, Nana?" Merryn asked eagerly.

"Yes, what are we doing?" Ferg echoed.

"What do you usually do?" Delia inquired.

"Ah, we usually start with warm-up exercises," Ferg replied.

He led them through relaxation and voice exercises of a basic kind that Delia herself preferred. The children struggled to contain their laughter during the silent scream exercise.

"What's the plan for the troupe?" Delia asked. "Are you putting on another play soon?"

"Well, that could be up to you, of course," Ferg said. "If you take up the opportunity."

"Why don't we do something little and fun? Maybe we could all pretend to be fairy tale witches, just for a game."

There was much cackling that ensued, and Delia felt uplifted. She had so much fun she forgot all about her apprehensions about the theatre and about being roped into doing something. She felt her shoulders relax as she and the children pretended to fly around on brooms and stir cauldrons with the other members.

"Well, that was cathartic," Kitty observed as they left. "I haven't experienced anything like that in quite some time."

"It was, wasn't it?" Delia agreed. "Laughter is good for the soul."

"Well, my soul has had quite a feast of it," Kitty said, her stomach rumbling. "And now I'm hungry for dinner and a couple of cocktails."

19

DECLAN

Snowflakes drifted lazily from the grey sky, blanketing the outskirts of Myrtlewood in a pristine layer of white. Declan, wrapped in a dark cloak, walked along the edge of the forest, his boots leaving deep impressions in the snow. The cold bit at his skin, but it was a sensation he barely noticed. The chill in his heart was far more ominous.

Memories of his past played like sombre cello music. The servitude to which he was bound, an unyielding chain, seemed more oppressive with each passing day.

Then there was Delia Spark...

His mind focused back on the encounter with the Crones at the pub. Declan felt a bitter twist in his gut. The rejection, the suspicion in their eyes – it stung.

She didn't understand.

How could she? As far as he knew, there was no one else in the world like him, cursed into an endless, solitary life.

The solitude of the wilderness was usually a refuge from chaos, but now it offered him little comfort.

A sharp caw pierced the silence of the waning afternoon. Startled, he looked up to see a raven perched on a bare branch, its black feathers stark against the white landscape. The bird's dark eyes met his own with an almost human-like understanding, an omen of loss. The raven cocked its head, observing him intently, as if it could see through the centuries that shrouded his soul.

Declan couldn't help but feel a strange kinship with the creature – both outcasts, observers of the world from their solitary perches.

The raven suddenly spread its wings and took flight, gliding effortlessly over the snow-covered forest.

Declan watched as it soared, admiring its freedom and grace. In that moment, the bird seemed to embody a message, urging him to rise above despair into a new perspective.

With a deep, contemplative sigh, Declan turned his gaze back to the path ahead.

His thoughts were interrupted by a sudden vision that flashed before his eyes – Delia Spark, falling through the sky. The image was so vivid, it stole his breath. Delia was in danger.

Despite his tangled emotions towards her, a sense of responsibility surged within him – the desire to protect her. It was a feeling he couldn't quite understand, yet it gnawed at him persistently.

The world around him had momentarily blurred, giving way to the vision. The world re-formed around him but the image remained etched in his mind: Delia's face etched with terror.

The details were hazy, like a dream slipping through fingers, but the sense of impending peril was unmistakable. Her eyes, wide with alarm, beseeched him silently.

She might have cast him out of the pub, but she wasn't getting rid of him that easily.

Declan's hand instinctively went to the seer's stone in his pocket.

The message from The Shepherd replayed in his mind – an ultimatum, a command to capture Delia and hand her over to the Order.

Declan clenched his fist around the stone, fury boiling inside him. The Crimson Shepherd's threat to ensure the Order never released him from his contract if he didn't comply echoed in his ears.

He couldn't help but wonder what had happened to the Cleric, who, despite everything, had seemed more human than the Shepherd.

Declan stopped in his tracks, gazing out over the snow-covered landscape. He knew he had to take action, but it was a choice between betraying himself or betraying her: handing Delia over to the Order, achieving the freedom he'd been seeking, or putting her life first – this woman he hardly knew – and risking his own.

The Order was powerful, and they'd offered him a way out,

along with a stream of other shiny promises. All he had to do was follow their instructions and betray the woman who wanted nothing more than to see him burn, anyway.

The decision should have been a simple one, yet it was anything but.

With renewed determination, Declan turned back towards the town. Delia might have awakened his long-dormant emotions, but it wasn't life and feeling he craved, it was nothingness.

20

DELIA

The children had just settled in to watch a fairy-tale film that Kitty had found for them, and Delia was looking forward to a few moments of quiet. Having them around had been marvellous, of course, but they were also running her off her feet a little.

It was fortunate that her newly boosted powers had given her more energy than she'd had before. Not only that, they'd all but eradicated the usual aches and pains in her hips and shoulders. She was becoming quite a fan of this magic business.

Despite the cold weather, they'd been out and about that morning. While Merryn and Keyne had played happily in the park in their winter coats, Delia had pondered what on earth was going to happen next.

She still didn't have any idea how to get hold of her family Grimoire; as far as she knew, the Bracewells weren't about to hand it over. And while she had promised Marjie a trip to York-shire to help in her own quest and visit her brother, she couldn't very well do that while Merryn and Keyne were visiting. She wanted to enjoy this time with them, even though the swings in the park held far less excitement for her, especially on a crisp winter morning, than they did for the eager young people.

As the movie began, Delia heard a knock at the door. "I'll get it," she said, as Kitty was already snuggled up with a blanket and popcorn on the couch next to the kids.

The woman who stood on her doorstep looked vaguely familiar. It took a moment to place her. "Mathilda?"

"You remembered!" said the woman, clutching her silver plait which hung over her shoulder and looking entirely too young in expression to be the age that her wrinkled face revealed she must be.

There was something naive about her, charming almost. As far as Delia knew, Mathilda was raised in the confines of some kind of spiritual convent. It seemed a parallel, similar but also opposite to how the Order were meant to live.

Surely, if the Veiled Sisterhood were the opposite of the Order, they must be good rather than evil, but something about them gave Delia pause. Perhaps it was the history that she only knew the briefest snippets of: Ingrid had been raised there and had left for good reason. Either way, her sister was here now, and perhaps Delia could find out more.

"Why are you here?" Delia asked.

Mathilda looked meek. "May I come in out of the cold?"

Delia glanced around, not wanting to disturb the film. "Come through to the sun porch," she said, ushering her in. "Would you like some tea?"

"No, thank you. I just had some," said Mathilda.

Delia nodded. "So, what is it? Why are you here?" she asked gently, as they settled into their chairs. She didn't want to seem rude. After all, Mathilda had helped them hide from the Order. But she needed to know what was going on.

"Our oracles tell us that something terrible is afoot," Mathilda said. "I come with a warning for you and the other Crones."

"Why did you come to me in particular?" Delia asked, curious.

"I decided to visit all of you," Mathilda admitted. "I can't say I've had the warmest reception so far."

"Have you seen Ingrid yet?"

Mathilda shook her head. "I'm summoning the courage to visit my sister. You must understand, she's not the easiest person in the world to get along with."

"As we well know," said Delia warmly. "However, she is a treasure."

"That she is," said Mathilda, her voice resigned.

"Can you tell us any more about these threats?" Delia asked.

Mathilda cleared her throat. "The oracles say that the darkest powers of the Order will rise as they have before in history, and soon there will be devastation, much worse than the last time."

Delia shivered slightly, though the sunporch was perfectly warm. "What happened the last time?"

Mathilda lowered her voice. "You may have heard rumours of the Witch Trials."

"Rumours!" said Delia. "That mark is well-etched in history. The witch burnings..."

Mathilda nodded solemnly. "It will be worse."

Delia's heart shuddered. She'd often thought the Order were bumbling and unorganised, though sometimes she'd suspected that this was an act to get the Crones to drop their guard, but they were clearly far more calculated and devious than she ever realised.

Their buffoonery clearly was an act, catching people off guard. Delia pondered this sham of her marriage, the strategy, the manipulation, the deceit. She wondered if she was still now being played. What if all the Order's actions had been deliberate, even their defeats?

"Is there any more you can tell us?" Delia asked.

Mathilda shook her head. "I'm not sure of the specifics. I'm sorry. However, understand that it will happen soon in the new year. You must act swiftly. You need to locate the other dragons."

Delia exhaled slowly. "You know about the dragons?"

Delia, herself, only knew one dragon personally, who was rather conveniently disguised as a puppy, but she needed to find out what more Mathilda knew.

"Of course, they are legend, and all legend is true in its way," Mathilda said. "Long ago, dragons roamed the earth, but were hunted to near extinction. The first Elemental Crones of Myrtlewood sought to save them. They worked together with the Druids and fae to open a new realm for the dragons, to save their kind. In return, the dragons – wise and powerful creatures that they were – gifted each crone the power to call upon their elemental dragons, hidden within this realm so that no one else can reach them."

"I didn't know all that," said Delia. "It makes sense, though...in a way. So the dragons were locked away safely, to be summoned by the Crones in times of need? Is that it?"

Mathilda nodded. "And this is such a time, unfortunately. But you are not alone in facing the challenges ahead. We're here – the Sisterhood, I mean. We're here to offer our help and our support."

"Thank you," said Delia, though she felt somewhat reserved. She couldn't speak on behalf of the other Crones, and really, Ingrid was closer to the Sisterhood than any of the rest of them, whether she liked it or not.

"This is a special token," said Mathilda, placing a small brown pouch on the coffee table in front of them. "You can use it if you need to contact us. Just rub it, and we will be able to find you. We can use magic. We are powerful, though we don't often show it."

Delia nodded, unsure of whether to take the gift or refuse it. She didn't feel entitled to do either. So she let it sit on the coffee table. "Why don't you give it to Ingrid?"

"I will...I have more of these, one for each of you," Mathilda explained.

"Alright then," said Delia. "Thank you."

"I'm in town for a few days, not long. I will visit Ingrid, perhaps..." Mathilda's words trailed off. "Perhaps you might want to take refuge in the Clochar. We would support you, of course. We would help you to master your powers."

Delia wondered how much Mathilda knew about their powers and how they had been playing up recently. "I'm not sure what Ingrid would think about that. Besides, I have family here. I have responsibilities."

"I understand, family is important," said Mathilda. "I only wish that Ingrid...Never mind. There's a lot of history, you understand."

"The reason she left?" Delia prompted.

Mathilda shook her head. "It was confusing at the time. I'm only beginning to understand now that there's so much more at stake than just our families. The whole world is at risk, you see."

It was a sobering thought and Delia did indeed see the risk. She'd seen more chaos and danger in the last few weeks than ever before in her life. More drama than in any theatre production she'd ever witnessed.

"I'll talk to the others," she promised Mathilda. "I'll see what they think."

"Thank you," said Mathilda, her eyes lighting up. "And I'll leave you now to your family." She stood to leave. "And thank you for listening," she said as Delia showed her out.

Delia wondered whether the Sisterhood could indeed be helpful, despite Ingrid's reservations. Would they all be safer at the Cloister? Perhaps, but they could not just up and leave. Besides, something told her there were other adventures in store for them that could not be carried out behind the closed walls of the Sisterhood's base, no matter how powerful and divine they might be.

She turned back to the grandkids, Mathilda's words ringing in her mind: all of them were at risk, not just her family, but a far greater risk, a far greater threat. Instead of joining them for the film, Delia called Marjie. They needed to talk this out.

21

DELIA

It wasn't long before Marjie and Agatha arrived. The children had just gotten to the part of the movie where the princess had escaped her tower when Delia had to excuse herself and usher a friendly-looking Marjie and a bitter, sour-faced Agatha to the sun porch, closing the doors so as not to disturb the film.

"So, that Mathilda, busybody she is, has called on you too, I gather," said Agatha, taking a seat.

"Did she go to you first?" Delia asked.

"I ran into her at the pub, didn't I?" said Agatha.

"I see," said Delia.

"And she called in at the tea shop," Marjie added. "She's a sweet girl, that one. Now, I know she's a fully-grown woman and not a girl, but I want to call her a girl because she's so young."

"She grew up cloistered in that strange cult setting. That's why she seems innocent as a child," said Agatha.

"That was my impression too," said Delia. "Tea?" she offered.

Marjie nodded. Delia returned a few moments later with tea and a small bottle of sherry, which seemed to brighten Agatha's mood only slightly.

As they sipped the tea and sherry, they compared notes on their recent visitor and Delia filled them in on the legends relating to the elemental dragons.

"I knew it!" said Agatha. "I will find the air dragon – a dragon of my very own!" she crowed delightedly, like a child receiving an unexpected puppy.

Delia couldn't help but smile. "I'm not sure Ingrid feels the earth dragon is hers; it's more the other way around!"

"Still...it is marvellous to think of more dragons, isn't it?" said Marjie. "Just imagine – a whole realm just for them, created by the early Crones in our lineage! It makes me glow with pride!"

"If Mathilda is to be trusted, anyway," Delia pointed out. "She did seem rather earnest, but perhaps she only knows part of the story."

"She told you both a lot more about these impending threats than she told me," Agatha grumbled.

"Perhaps because *we* gave her a chance to talk," Marjie jibed.

"I guess she still hasn't visited Ingrid yet," said Agatha. "Very suspicious."

"I don't know," said Delia. "I can't say I automatically trust the Sisterhood, but Mathilda seems so harmless."

"They did help us," Marjie reminded them. "When we needed it."

"And they want to help us again, whether we like it or not, by the sounds of it," said Agatha.

"Did she give you a stone too, for summoning the Order?" Delia asked.

"She tried," said Agatha.

"Me too," said Marjie, holding up a small pouch similar to the one Delia had set on the table. Agatha eyed it suspiciously. "Ingrid's not going to like it, I'm sure."

"She isn't," Delia agreed. "She seems to have a lot of baggage when it comes to that lot, including her own family."

"Don't we all," said Marjie cheerfully, though there was an obvious sadness underneath the cheer.

"I came across something in my Grimoire," Agatha said. "And I can't help but return to it over and over again: *Whenne elders blaze, the soth shal rise, In starlit e'en and moonlit skies.*"

"Oh, that's an old song," said Marjie. "Except it's different." She began to sing. "*When elders blaze, the truth shall rise, 'neath stars and moon that grace our skies...*"

"Yours is a more modern adaptation, no doubt," said Agatha. "But come to think of it, I do remember the tune."

"What do you think it means? And why do you think it's relevant now?" Delia asked. "Ingrid has an old elder tree in her garden. I wonder if it's connected somehow."

"There are elder trees all over this part of the world," said Agatha. "I don't see why it would be related."

"I don't know; it was special, I'm sure of that," said Delia. "She showed it to me that first night when I got lost in the woods trying to visit her house. There was something so majestic about it, something wise and ancient."

"Now who's waxing poetic," said Agatha, rolling her eyes.

"Excuse me, loves, I just need to pop to the loo," Marjie said.

Delia couldn't help but wonder whether Marjie had excused herself to give Delia and Agatha a moment alone.

"You're right, Agatha, you seem troubled. More than usual," said Delia.

Agatha blustered. "It's nothing really."

"How could it be nothing if it's upsetting *you*?" Delia asked poignantly.

"Oh, very well, if you must know...It seems our dear friend Covvey has taken an interest in you."

"Oh..." said Delia. She shrugged. "I don't think....I mean... I'm not really in the market for a relationship. I'm feeling quite happy on my own. And he's probably not my type." Thoughts rushed through her head, a potential list of reasons, a rationale that might stop Agatha from being so bothered. Clearly, she and Covvey were close.

"It's not your fault," Agatha conceded. "It's just we have been such good friends, Covvey and I."

"And I wouldn't want anything getting in the way of that,"

Delia assured her. "I appreciate Covvey, but I barely know him at all. If you like him so much, why don't you tell him?"

Agatha shook her head. "I'm not much one for affections of an intimate nature. Our friendship is close. We talk about all manner of things; we confide in each other."

"And you've never wanted anything more than that?" Delia asked.

"Well, what more is there really to want?" said Agatha. "I'm not exactly a romantic sort. Do you understand?"

"Even if you're not," Delia said, "there is something special about your friendship. Couldn't you make it clear to him? That he's important to you?"

Agatha stiffened. "It sounds awfully vulnerable. And I don't like being vulnerable."

"Sometimes we need to be vulnerable," said Delia. "Otherwise, we go around in circles, over the same nonsense over and over. We never get anywhere that way," Delia pointed out.

"Have you been peeking inside my head?" Agatha asked sternly, and then her face cracked into a smile. "Oh, you're alright, Delia Spark. I don't have any bone to pick with you, not really. I only wish..."

"Wishing isn't much good if it's not accompanied by action," Delia suggested. "You could just let him know that he's special to you – or not. It's your own choice!" she added, as Agatha shot her a sharp glance.

"At least I know you're not conspiring to steal him from me." Agatha said it begrudgingly.

At that moment, Marjie returned. "Have you gotten anywhere with that Elders Blaze song?...Or poem, whichever way you prefer it."

"I don't understand why it's standing out for you, in particular," said Delia. "Just because you saw it in your grimoire?"

Agatha cleared her throat. "If you must know, my powers are rather – chaotic – at the moment. I believe I've suggested as much."

Delia nodded for her to continue.

"Well, the other day, all the books flew around in the air... all around the library, and it's not the first time. Absolute nightmare! So chaotic! Anyway, when I finally sorted it out and charmed everything back into place—"

"Wait, you can do that?" Delia interrupted. "I'm sorry, go on, but you must teach me how to tidy up with magic!"

Agatha sighed and continued. "When all was tidied away, my grimoire was opened to a page about some kind of cloud, and then the pages began to move as it sat there on the table, until they stopped right at that very poem."

"Elder is a tree of transitions," Marjie mused. "She guards the borders between worlds."

Agatha chuckled. "A bit like Marjie trying to navigate a conversation without landing in hot water."

"Oh, please, Agatha. If we're talking about navigating, let's not forget your outrageous driving, or your uncanny ability to transition from tea to the stronger brews without batting an eye. But, speaking of the elder tree, she sings, did you know?"

"Sings?" Delia asked, incredulous.

Agatha nudged Marjie. "Much like you, except the tree's probably more in tune."

Marjie giggled. "At least I'm brave enough to try," she added. "But legend has it that the elder's magical song can soothe the soul or set it ablaze with energy. Elder also has a dual nature, much like your cooking offers the promise of nourishment but always teeters on the brink of disaster."

Agatha feigned offense. "My cooking aside, the elder tree does demand wisdom and respect. Approach with caution, or face the consequences."

Marjie turned to Delia. "Oh yes, and the most important thing to remember is never to burn the elder tree – not only because its smoke can be toxic, but because it is said to unleash curses."

"That was part of the legend, wasn't it?" Agatha said, leaning back in her chair, her hand reaching to her jaw as she pondered. "The sacred elder grove...?"

"Oh yes," Marjie added. "Don't you recall, Delia? We told you about the ancient curse. The witch who was murdered..."

"I'm sure it was something to do with that wretched cat," said Agatha.

"Mephistos?" Delia asked.

Agatha nodded. "Isn't that what he told us – though I doubt he can be trusted at all. Didn't he brag that he was a demon that was unleashed at that time?"

"I believe so," said Marjie. "But didn't it all happen in an elder grove?"

Agatha's eyes widened. "Oh...right, it did. Blast it all. It's so obvious."

"Do you think we need to go there?" Delia asked. "Could it hold some clue? Would it even still be there after all these years?"

Agatha shrugged. "The elder grove may or may not still exist, and it might all just be a lot of hot air. But it's worth investigating."

Delia turned to Marjie. "I know I said I'd go with you to Yorkshire after the new year, when the kids return to Gillian, but..."

"But perhaps this takes precedent," said Marjie, smiling, though her eyes still betrayed sadness. "I've made no inroads connecting with my brother anyway."

Delia sighed and patted Marjie on the shoulder. "There's nothing to be done for now."

"In the meantime, the elders are calling," said Agatha. "And it turns out I'm brave enough to sing with them after all!" She burst into a rather off-tune version of the song that Marjie had just sung. But not knowing the words herself, she improvised with humming and random additions until the three of them were cackling uncontrollably.

When elders blaze, the truth shall rise, and sherry pours forth from the skies!

. . .

"Well, I dare say, elders aside, I have been feeling rather energised lately," said Marjie. "Haven't you?"

Delia nodded. "And I've needed it, with the kids around."

"A little too much energy if you ask me," Agatha grumbled.

"I think it's a sign that we're due for another adventure," Marjie said firmly. "We'd better talk to Ingrid."

22

INGRID

The wind carried a sense of anticipation, stirring the leaves erratically. Ingrid stood at the edge of her cottage, her eyes closed as she listened to the whispers of the forest. The trees spoke a language only she could understand, a language of rustling leaves and creaking branches. Today, they murmured of a change in the air, a disturbance in the natural rhythm of the woods.

As she stood there, the forest seemed to lean in. Someone was coming.

The crows cawed from their perches on the roof of her hut, their calls echoing through the trees.

She opened her eyes, gazing into the woods. The leaves rustled again, more insistently this time, as if urging her to prepare. Ingrid knew the forest did not speak idly; its warnings were always for a reason. Someone was coming, someone whose footsteps were already woven into her past.

Drawing a deep breath, Ingrid turned back towards her cottage. The fire needed stoking, and she had herbs to prepare. If the forest was right, if someone from her past was indeed on their way, she needed to be ready for whatever that reunion might bring.

Moments later, Ingrid was standing in her cottage, the air thick with the scent of herbs and the warmth of a crackling fire, when she heard a knock at the door. She opened it to find her own sister standing there, her usually neat braids a frazzled mess, her expression anxious.

"Mathilda? What is it?" Ingrid asked. "What brings you all the way out here?"

Mathilda wasted no time. "Dark forces are brewing, Ingrid. The Crones are at risk. The Sisterhood wants to offer help."

Ingrid's expression remained stoic, her voice steady. "I'm perfectly capable of taking care of myself, as are the other Crones. We don't need the Sisterhood's help."

"I thought you'd say as much..." Mathilda looked around. "It's beautiful out here, but you always did love nature. Do you remember the Clochar gardens, Ingrid? How you used to light up among the flowers and herbs?"

Ingrid's response was tinged with bitterness. "I couldn't wait to get out of that place. It was a cage, not a sanctuary."

Mathilda lowered her gaze.

Ingrid sighed. "I don't mean to upset you. I never mean to do that."

"No, but you resent my home, my entire world," Mathilda said, gazing at Ingrid with sad eyes. "Don't you remember the good times? You and Gwyneth..."

Ingrid felt a surge of old emotions – sorrow, betrayal. "She turned against me in the end," she said quietly, her voice heavy with unspoken stories.

Mathilda countered softly, "Gwyneth would argue it was you who turned against the Sisterhood. You left...you left me."

Ingrid's heart shuddered a little as it traversed this painful territory. "I did what I had to do, Mathilda. There's no point in circling back over the past endlessly. It's ancient history."

"But you loved the Clochar, remember?" Mathilda pressed gently. "I remember how you used to be, in the gardens..."

Ingrid shook her head slowly, her face a canvas of sadness and regret. "There are things you do not understand, Mathilda. Things that happened, things that changed me."

Mathilda's expression darkened with a hint of something more, a secret or knowledge that Ingrid couldn't decipher.

She wondered what her sister was hiding but chose not to press further. Instead, she decided to offer Mathilda a cup of tea. After all, they were family, and that did matter on some level, despite everything.

*And it's probably wise not to get on the bad side of the Sisterhood...*Ingrid thought. She had learned that truth the hard way.

Ingrid gestured to her sister to sit by the fire.

Mathilda sat down, her hands clasped tightly in her lap, in contrast to Ingrid's more relaxed posture as she moved about the room, preparing tea. Ingrid's mind drifted between past and present, choices made and paths taken. The connection with her sister, strained and complex, was still a bond that she valued, even if it pained her at times. Besides, Mathilda had come to their aid not long ago.

Outside, the wind howled softly, a lonely sound that seemed to echo Ingrid's thoughts.

Mathilda broke the silence. "I have something for you." She reached into her cloak and pulled out a small brown pouch. She held it out to Ingrid.

When Ingrid did not take it Mathilda opened the pouch slightly, revealing a small stone nestled within. "It's a summoning stone."

Ingrid eyed the object warily, her instinct to refuse the offer. "Mathilda, I don't need..."

But Mathilda interrupted gently, "Please, just keep it. It's just in case you change your mind. If you need help, call on us."

Ingrid looked at the stone, its surface smooth and unassuming, yet pulsing with a latent power she knew all too well. She reached out slowly, her fingers brushing against the soft suede before drawing back.

Mathilda pressed the pouch into Ingrid's hand, closing her fingers around it. "I will always be there for you, Ingrid. This is my promise to you."

The weight of the pouch in her hand felt heavier than its size would suggest.

Ingrid looked up at Mathilda, her sister's face illuminated by the flickering light of the fire. There was a sincerity there, a genuine concern that Ingrid couldn't ignore.

"Thank you, Mathilda," she said quietly. "I'll keep it...just in case."

As Mathilda left the cottage, Ingrid sat alone by the fire, watching the flames. Their glow cast a comforting yet haunting light across the room, illuminating her thoughts and reviving memories long buried.

In the fire, she saw flickers of a younger self, of days when life in the Clochar was not just a discipline but a haven of adventure. In her mind's eye, a face appeared: Gwyneth, her eyes as bright as the stars above them on those long nights they had spent together, hidden away from the world. They were young then, brimming with the naivety of youth. Their love was a secret nurtured in the shadows of the Clochar's walls.

But the memory of that warmth was quickly overshadowed by the cold, tearing pain of betrayal. Gwyneth chose the Sisterhood over her. Ingrid remembered the look in Gwyneth's eyes as she revealed the truth, that she'd reported Ingrid's various transgressions to the elder Sisters. It was true that Gwyneth would never have snuck out of the Clochar grounds without encouragement, but the betrayal had devastated Ingrid.

That day, a part of Ingrid had broken, a fracture that never truly healed.

Now Gwyneth was an elder herself. Ingrid wondered what that said about her, about the choices she had made, the paths she had walked. Had Gwyneth ever regretted her decision? Did she ever look into the fire and see their shared past flickering in its depths?

And then there was Mathilda, caught in the web of the

Sisterhood's machinations. Ingrid could see the conflict in Mathilda's eyes, the struggle between duty and doubt. Perhaps their warnings were worthy of careful consideration, after all; danger did seem to shroud the Myrtlewood Crones, but help from the Sisterhood would come at a cost, a balancing of scales in their grand design. Poor Mathilda, so earnest and yet so unaware of the deeper currents she was wading into.

Ingrid's thoughts drifted to what she had glimpsed all those years ago in the mountains, a secret so chilling it still sent shivers down her spine. She still didn't understand it, she only knew instinctively that something was dreadfully wrong. It was a glimpse into the heart of the Sisterhood that had compelled her to leave. She wondered if Mathilda would ever see the Sisterhood for what it truly was, or if she, like Gwyneth, would be lost to their cause.

Ingrid shook herself. She was at peace with her life now, for the most part.

The fire crackled and Ingrid let out a long, slow breath. There was no going back, only forward, into whatever unknowns might await.

23

THE SHEPHERD

F ather Benedict descended the curving staircase, his mind racing with the indignity of the Elders' rebuke. The cold stone walls of the tower echoed his mounting rage. Outside, the night had fallen over the compound. The moon hung low in the sky, as if smirking at him. He paused, his breath visible in the crisp air, as he contemplated the gravity of the situation.

Each step Father Benedict took resonated through the cold, damp air. The walls, slick with the moisture of the night, reflected the flickering torchlight.

He had come to warn the Elders of imminent threat, and yet they had dismissed his concerns. Did they not see? The awakening of the Veiled Sisterhood was not just a threat; it was a harbinger of change, a challenge to the very foundations of the Order of Crimson.

As Father Benedict continued his descent, his mind replayed the harsh words of the Elders.

Elder Mordant, cold and unyielding, had glared at him. "You overstep your bounds, Shepherd. It is not your place to dictate the unleashing of powers."

"But the threat is real, Elders. The Sisterhood's magic is unlike anything we've faced. We must act!" Father Benedict replied, struggling to keep his composure.

Elder Firth, his spectacles reflecting the dim light, added sternly, "Your zeal blinds you, Benedict. You forget your place. The Order has stood for centuries without your impudence."

"The Sisterhood's awakening changes everything," Father Benedict insisted. "We risk everything by waiting!"

Elder Quill, always quick to anger, retorted, "Do not lecture us on risk, Shepherd! You dare to assume authority that is not yours. Your arrogance is a danger to us all."

"I only seek to protect the Order, to do what is necessary," Father Benedict insisted.

Elder Burrow, the eldest, spoke last, his voice a weary but firm rebuke. "Your 'necessary' is a path to chaos. Remember the Cleric, Benedict. Remember his fate for defying the Order's will."

A black rage seeped through Father Benedict's defences. The cleric had defied him, defied the will of the Almighty. In his role as the Crimson Shepherd, Benedict had been the one to dole out punishment. How dare the Elders threaten him now?

A tumultuous cascade of thoughts besieged him. *Years of servitude, and yet they doubt me at every turn.*

As the rage stagnated into cold resentment, Father Benedict realised the futility of his pleas. The Elders, set in their ways, would not be moved by his urgency. As he left the chamber, their words continued to haunt him.

Their complacency will be their own undoing.

A memory unbidden came to him, a day many years ago when Elder Mordant had placed a firm hand on his shoulder, speaking words of rare praise. "Your dedication is the backbone of our Order, Benedict," he had said. How distant that moment seemed now, buried under layers of disappointment and unheeded warnings.

As he crossed the threshold into the night, a young novice, cloaked in the Order's colours, approached, a look of reverence in his eyes. "Father Benedict, is all well?" he asked timidly.

"All is as the Almighty wills," Benedict replied curtly.

They may doubt me, but they know not what I am capable of.

Crossing into the main courtyard, he looked up at the tallest tower from which he'd just retreated; the spire where the Elders resided loomed over him like a judgmental sentinel. *They sit in their lofty positions,* Benedict thought bitterly, *detached from the realities of the world below. They do not understand the urgency, the necessity of action.*

In the gardens, the night bloomed with the scent of the resinous clary sage the monks here often used for incense, a reminder of the sacredness of the Mission. But to Father Benedict, it was now a scent tainted with the stagnation of the Elders' inaction. He walked through the gardens, each step fuelling his resolve.

The Almighty must triumph but the Order must first evolve, to take decisive steps, or we will be overtaken by the very forces we seek to control.

In the shadows, he could see the faint outlines of various novices and acolytes, scurrying about their nightly duties, oblivious to the storm brewing within their ranks.

They trusted in the wisdom of the Elders. But Benedict knew better now. It was time for a new direction, a new leader who understood the true nature of the battle they faced.

He reached the edge of the gardens, the cool night air brushing against his face; a sinister smile crept upon his lips.

The Elders might have dismissed him, but they had under-estimated his power.

He would show them, he would show them all. The supremacy of the Almighty was not just a tool to be wielded by the Elders; it was a force that he, Father Benedict, was destined to bear.

As Father Benedict disappeared into the night, the wind began to rise, rustling through the trees of the Order's gardens. It was as if the very earth sensed the change. The Order was on the cusp of a storm the Elders had never foreseen.

24
INGRID

S he was running alongside Gwyneth, their laughter echoing through the hills, the grass a vibrant green beneath them, the air filled with the scent of wildflowers and the earthy aroma of damp soil.

"Race you to the top!" Gwyneth called out, her voice light and teasing.

"You're on!" Ingrid replied, her heart pounding with excitement. She could feel the wind in her hair, the rush of adrenaline coursing through her veins.

They scrambled up the mountainside, shrugging off the strict rules and conventions of the Clochar. The sky above them darkened, clouds gathering ominously, but they paid it no heed, lost in their moment of freedom.

As they crested the hill, an enormous structure peeked above the skyline, unlike anything Ingrid had ever seen, ornate, crystalline, and shimmering in the fading light. It seemed ancient and other-worldly.

As they approached the structure, Ingrid felt tiny in comparison. It rose, a disk of gemstones and runes, far taller than any building she'd seen in her sheltered life. She felt a tug in her heart, as if it held answers to questions she hadn't yet formed.

"We shouldn't be here, Ingrid," Gwyneth whispered, her voice quivering. "The elders won't forgive this."

"But why must we always follow without question?" Ingrid retorted, her voice laced with curiosity and defiance. "There's more to our world than what they tell us."

"Ingrid! Gwyneth!"

They were no longer alone. An elder sister from the Clochar, cloaked in robes that seemed to absorb the light around her, appeared before them.

"Young ones," she scolded, her voice cold. "You know you are not permitted here."

Ingrid, her curiosity piqued, stepped forward. "But why? What is this place?"

Gwyneth tugged at her sleeve. "Ingrid, leave it. It's not our place to question."

But Ingrid couldn't help herself. "I don't understand. Why must everything be so secret?"

The elder's gaze hardened. "Your disobedience will not go unpunished. And as for your questions, you would do well to trust in the Sisterhood."

Ingrid felt a pang of frustration, the elder's words echoing in her *mind. Even Gwyneth seemed to have succumbed to the unquestioning loyalty the Clochar demanded.*

When the elder scolded them, Ingrid's shame was obliterated by the rebellious fire stirring within her. She looked at the elder, her eyes brimming with unshed tears, not of sorrow, but of frustration.

Ingrid's gaze was drawn to a faint glimmering light emanating from a small, hidden alcove within the structure. For a fleeting second, she thought she saw the silhouette of a figure, cloaked in shadows.

As the elder lectured them, Ingrid's vision blurred, and for a moment, she saw a different realm, a vast landscape stretching under a starlit sky, where a grove of trees stood, branches swaying as if whispering ancient secrets. She blinked, and the vision vanished as quickly as it had appeared.

"I just want to know the truth," Ingrid insisted.

The elder sister glared at her. "Beware, for not all truths bring comfort."

Ingrid felt a chill run down her spine, a premonition of a different life altogether, one not dictated by the Sisterhood, but only confined by the limits of her own imagination.

"What lies beyond the Clochar?" Ingrid asked, her voice barely above a whisper. The elder turned away, leaving her question hanging in the air.

The atmosphere was charged with an energy that both frightened and exhilarated her. She could no longer blindly follow a community that cloaked itself in mystery and refused to quench her thirst for knowledge. The boundaries of the Clochar had become a prison and her soul screamed out for escape.

. . .

Ingrid jerked awake from a restless slumber, her heart racing. A strange, ethereal light seeped through the window, casting dancing shadows across the room. With cautious movements, she eased out of bed, her bare feet touching the cold, wooden floor. Each step was deliberate, a silent invocation to the protective spirits of her hut.

Approaching the window, she peered out into the night. The elder tree in her back garden, usually a dark shadow in the night, was ablaze with an unearthly glow.

Its branches seemed to be alight with a flame.

Ingrid's heart pounded as she hurried downstairs, her hands brushing against the rough, wooden banister.

The air was cool and crisp, filled with the night's stillness, broken only by the soft creaking of the old hut. She reached the door, her hand hesitating on the latch. Taking a deep breath to steady her nerves, she opened it.

Outside, Ingrid breathed a sigh of relief. There was no fire. The world was bathed in darkness, the glowing spectacle of the elder tree now absent. Only the stars above shone down, their light a dim, comforting presence. Ingrid stepped out, her feet sinking into the dew-laden grass, the night air enveloping her in its embrace.

She walked towards the elder tree, its form now just the familiar shadow in the darkness. Her hand reached out, tentatively touching the rough bark. At her touch, the tree began to glow once again, its light soft and warm, like the embers of a long-burning fire.

The air around her hummed with an ancient melody, a song she had learned as a child. It was a tune sung by the elders of her community, a song of protection and wisdom that was said to be as old as the hills. The notes seemed to emanate from the tree itself, the sound weaving around her like a comforting blanket.

Ingrid closed her eyes, allowing the melody to wash over her.

When elders blaze, the truth shall rise, 'neath stars and moon that grace our skies.

Their words ignite, like ancient flames, foretelling life's untold reframes.

Upon their brows, each furrowed line, a prophecy of age's sign,

Speaking of a time when dark and light, in amity, will reunite.

These sagas old, with depth profound, through silent ages, they resound.

A time foreseen, when shadow meets the day, in dance, their strife will fade away.

Their voices, like a chapel's bell, through time's vast corridor do swell,

Heralding a day when rifts will mend, and in their wisdom, we ascend.

. . .

So hark, the elder's lore, attend, within their tales, our fates portend.

For when they blaze with truth so clear, a new age of unity draws near.

A promise of a world restored, in their harmonious accord,

When light and dark, no longer foes, weave lore anew life free of woes.

It was an old song, with many versions, but as Ingrid stood there, singing softly, the words took on a new significance. The light from the tree enveloped her, the melody growing louder in her ears. Images flashed in her mind – memories of her childhood, lessons from her mentors, and glimpses of ancient rituals performed under the watchful eye of the elder tree. It was as if the tree was speaking to her, imparting wisdom and strength, reminding her of the deep connection she shared with the natural world.

The elder tree was, of course, known for its protective qualities and deep connection to the magical world. It was often said to be a guardian against malevolent forces, a symbol of transformation and rebirth, complete with many medical uses. It was an important plant in any witch's garden, but now it seemed to take on a new life, a deeper significance, a divine presence...

Ingrid felt a surge of energy coursing through her. As the

melody faded and the light dimmed, the tree stood silent once more, its glow gone, yet the feeling of power and connection lingered. Ingrid couldn't tell if it was a message of support or warning, but her instincts told her it was both.

25
DELIA

Merryn and Keyne insisted on going to Ingrid's hut with Delia, and since she only had a couple of days left with them before Gillian picked them up, she could hardly refuse.

The weather was drizzly as they approached with Marjie and Agatha in tow.

Delia was surprised to see that the door was open. She, Marjie, and Agatha exchanged uncertain glances.

"Well, what are you all standing there for?" said Ingrid's voice from behind them.

"How did you get there?" Merryn asked. "We just walked past you and I didn't see you at all!"

"Are you magic?" said Keyne, with a touch of wonder in his voice.

"Of course she's magic," said Merryn. "She's a forest witch, remember?"

"Oh," said Keyne playfully. "I hope she doesn't eat us for dinner."

"You're not to my taste," said Ingrid dryly, making both children giggle.

"What *are* you doing out here?" Agatha asked Ingrid.

"Well," said Ingrid, "I was waiting for you, and I decided to inspect the rosemary."

"And you left the door open, dear?" said Marjie.

"It does what it likes and it likes to wait for me sometimes, you know," Ingrid explained.

"I do indeed know," said Marjie. "I am fortunate to also live in a house that feels like a friend."

"I'd like a friendly house too," said Keyne. "I would like a big one on a mountain. Maybe a castle."

"I wanted a castle first," Merryn insisted. "Don't copy me."

As they all made their way inside, Keyne asked, "Where's the dragon puppy?"

"Dragon puppy?" Ingrid sighed. "He's out the back."

She led them to the back garden and the children and Torin scrambled ahead. Delia checked to see if they were okay. The dragon was safely in his puppy form, and the two dogs were chasing each other around the back garden, the children giggling.

"We need to keep an eye on them," said Delia.

"They'll be fine," said Agatha dismissively.

Delia frowned. "What if he turns back into a dragon and clobbers them all?"

"*She,* remember?" said Ingrid, with a protectiveness in her tone. "And don't worry. She seems to prefer to be a dog most of the time, these days." She sighed again. "I can't really tell a dragon what to do after all."

"If you can't, then there's no hope for the rest of us," Delia joked. She positioned herself near the window so that she could keep an eye on the children playing outside.

Over a cup of mugwort tea, all three visiting Crones told Ingrid about their encounters with her sister.

Ingrid sat quietly, listening. Delia had no doubt she was taking in all the details.

"Has she been to see you yet?" Agatha asked Ingrid.

"Briefly," said Ingrid, sounding as if she preferred not to talk about it.

"And what do you make of all this?" Delia asked. "Are the Sisterhood friend or foe?"

Ingrid shook her head. "I've thought about this for many years, you know, and I can't decide. All I know is that I left because they were covering up a great secret. It might have even been something good. But I had a feeling...not that it was evil—"

"What then?" asked Marjie.

Ingrid shrugged. "You know that feeling you get when you're in the presence of something enormous...tremendous. It was like that, and they wouldn't tell me anything about it. I felt betrayed. And from then on, I could never really consider myself a part of that cult or whatever it is."

"It's a strong word to use," Marjie said. "Who are we to judge their way of life?"

"Well, I figure I'm best placed to judge," Ingrid said, "since it was my way of life for my early years, many of them at any rate. They do take in struggling widows, solo mothers. That's why we went there after my father passed away..."

"That was good of them," said Delia, getting the distinct impression that Ingrid was only telling half of the story.

"I suppose so," said Ingrid, her voice softening. "My mother didn't last for too many more years. The Sisterhood raised us; they were our family, our everything."

"It must have been hard to leave," said Marjie, her eyes brimming with tears.

"It was a difficult decision, but I really didn't have a choice in the end," Ingrid said. "Once that separation occurred, I couldn't go back. I couldn't be kept in the dark, and I realised there was a whole world that I needed to explore. I couldn't stay there and live my life."

"Still...to leave all that behind. They were your family," said Marjie.

"That's enough of that conversation," Ingrid said sharply. "It's best not to dwell on the past. Now, here we are, in the present."

"What do you make of the Sisterhood's warning, then?" Delia asked.

"Dark powers rising? Sounds awfully ambiguous," Agatha muttered.

"Unfortunately, Mathilda is probably right about that," said Ingrid. "I can sense something in the forest. Something has changed. And I have at times felt like I was being watched, observed by a malevolent force of some sort. I can't explain that."

"Maybe you're being stalked by the same person Delia is," Agatha suggested. "That rogue tracker was at the pub the other night."

"Was he now?" Ingrid asked, with some interest. "What did he want?"

"I don't know," said Delia. "We told him to get out of town."

"He knows he's not welcome anymore, that's for sure," said Marjie. "Nobody working for the Order is, even if he's somehow not affected by the cloaking spell."

"It shows he's independent, at least," Delia said. She had never fully explained everything that had happened with Declan – that he was the one person who'd seen them at the abandoned hamlet when they'd rescued the ancient book, nor had she told her friends that the tracker had tried to stop her from walking into the Order's trap when she was determined to rescue Kitty. She'd kept this to herself, as it didn't seem right to tell them, like sharing a secret, though she wasn't sure entirely why.

"Perhaps he'll leave us alone now," said Marjie doubtfully.

Delia shrugged. Somehow, she didn't think so. There was

something about his eyes that bored into her soul, leaving her feeling vulnerable, exposed. She couldn't imagine a man of such intensity merely walking away.

"Right, onto other business," said Ingrid. "My elder tree was glowing like a lantern last night. I've never seen anything like it. It's always been a magical tree, but..."

"Oh, just like in Agatha's book," said Marjie.

"What's this now?" Ingrid asked, with the tone of a stern schoolmistress.

Agatha harumphed. "My powers played up and my grimoire opened to an old poem about the elder's blaze grove."

"There's a song too." Marjie began singing.

Ingrid raised her hand to silence her. "That was the very tune I heard last night as I placed my hand against the tree's bark."

A shiver ran through Delia and she wouldn't have been surprised if it were shared by everyone in that room.

"It feels like it's all coming together, doesn't it?" said Marjie. "Like these are clues placed for us, the ancient ones..."

"It doesn't mean we have to follow them," said Agatha. "What if they're deliberately leading us astray?"

"It doesn't seem like it," said Delia, looking out the window again to see the children still playing happily. "I think this is something bigger than that...at least it doesn't seem malevolent to me."

Marjie nodded. "No, nor to me."

"That's not all the news," said Ingrid. "I've managed to have some more chats with our dragon friend. It's not really a conversation in the usual sense. It's more feelings and occasional images and words. I keep getting an image of the sky... clouds."

"Sounds like the dragon's telling you to go fly a kite," said Agatha, chuckling.

"I sometimes get a feeling that resonates to the feeling of land or the earth."

"Well, that's paradoxical," Agatha mused. "What is it? The sky or the earth?"

"I'm not entirely sure," Ingrid said, "but perhaps we need to make a pilgrimage."

"A Crone pilgrimage!" Marjie beamed. "I do like the sound of that. Where will we be pilgriming to?"

"The sacred elder grove, of course," said Ingrid.

"So it is real?" Delia asked. The crones looked at her quizzically. "I mean, it's still there. It still exists?"

"Well, who knows," said Ingrid. "I have a sense of where it might be. There's even a map in the old grimoire that we retrieved."

"Now you're talking!" said Agatha. "I love a good map."

"You love a good *nap* too," said Marjie. "Especially after a few too many glasses of sherry."

Agatha glared at her in response while Ingrid went to fetch the book. She returned moments later, flipping through the pages until she found what she was looking for.

"Way up there, on the side of a mountain?" Agatha said, looking at the map that Delia could make no sense of at all.

"Indeed," said Ingrid. "The goats might be able to get us up there. They are nimble wee fellows."

"Perhaps you could use your wind power," Marjie said to Agatha. "I hear it's wreaking havoc in your house after all. You need an outlet."

"I don't know how to utilise it," said Agatha. "It's funny. I've never had that much affinity for wind before."

"I beg to differ. I've had the misfortune of being in your presence after you've eaten beans down at the pub!" Marjie said, chuckling.

"Right, you two, settle down," said Ingrid. "We have important business to discuss here, not just trading cheap insults."

"The children are with me for two more nights," said Delia. "After that, perhaps?"

"Perfect!" said Marjie. "A new year's Crone adventure."

Despite Marjie's enthusiasm, Delia couldn't help but feel a lead weight form in her gut, an instinctual reaction to impending danger.

26
DELIA

"Smells delicious," said Delia as the rich scent of red wine and herbs wafted through the house.

Kitty's famous beef Bourguignon was almost ready.

It was the end of the children's stay with Delia, and Gillian would arrive shortly to pick them up. But of course, Delia wanted her daughter to stay for dinner.

"I hope she eats this time," said Kitty. "She barely touched Christmas dinner. That's not like Gilly at all."

Delia shrugged. "I just wish she'd tell me what was going on."

"Hah!" said Kitty. "And yet think of all you haven't told her."

Delia sighed and walked over to the staircase. She called out to the children. "Are you all packed up?"

Merryn and Keyne had been sent to do their own packing.

Delia was sure they'd leave something behind and was prepared to go up and check on them. They'd spent the whole morning in the garden with their warm coats on, making a surprise for Delia. Kitty had supervised them and said it was something special.

"We're all done," said Merryn, coming down the stairs with her bag. Keyne was there too, dragging his bag behind him.

Delia checked and was surprised to find that they seemed to have taken all their belongings, aside from a couple of scarves and gloves strewn around the living room.

As she retrieved the final glove there was a knock at the door.

Torin barked.

"It's alright, love. It'll just be Gilly," said Delia. And she was right – it was indeed her daughter standing there, her strawberry blonde hair slightly frazzled. She still looked pale and drawn but stronger somehow. She smiled at Delia, who leaned forward to hug her, but Gillian grimaced.

"What is it, love?" asked Delia. "Are you in pain?"

"A little," said Gillian. "Just cramps. Nothing ghastly."

"Dinner's almost ready," Kitty called out from the kitchen.

Merryn and Keyne rushed to hug their mother.

"Did you have a nice trip with Nana?" Gilly asked.

"It was so much fun...it was magical," said Merryn.

Delia and Kitty shot each other amused but slightly concerned glances.

"We did a lot of good things," Keyne added. "We even made—"

"Shush, it's a surprise!" Merryn interrupted him.

"I can't wait to find out what you made for me," said Delia eagerly.

"Dinner's ready!" Kitty called.

Gillian smiled tensely. "I've brought my own, actually. I'm sorry...It smells amazing and you know I love your cooking, Kitty. I'm just on a special diet."

Kitty frowned. "You're not trying to lose weight, are you? You look fit enough."

Gillian waved her hand dismissively. "No, it's not that. I've just had some health issues lately and I'm on a special diet."

"It's fine, Gillian. What matters is that you're here," Delia replied, though she couldn't help but worry.

As they settled down for dinner, Gillian retrieved a container full of some kind of salad which she ate ravenously.

Delia raised her eyebrows and shrugged at Kitty as if to say: *at least she's eating.*

The children eagerly tucked into Kitty's delicious food.

"You should try this, Mummy. It's really good!" said Keyne.

"Mummy can't," said Merryn. "You heard her."

"The doctor said she might die!" Keyne said.

"No, she said *diet*. Which means a special way you eat...I think."

Delia smiled at her granddaughter. "That's right, dear. Mummy's just looking after her health."

Gillian put her fork down and cleared her throat. "I've had a lot of allergies," she explained. "I have to be very careful at the moment. There are so many things I have to avoid...you know?"

"Oh, I've been on one of those diets too," said Kitty.

Delia rolled her eyes at the memory of Kitty's dramatic elimination diet where she'd eaten nothing but rice and pears for weeks only, to discover the only issue she was really having was drinking too much whisky.

"I hope what you're eating helps," said Delia sincerely, observing the container of precisely diced vegetables.

Gillian nodded. "It seems to be good so far."

"You do look better, love," said Delia. "I must admit I was a little worried."

Gillian smiled. "Everything is okay. We're all going to be fine." It sounded like she was reassuring herself as much as the rest of them.

"I'm going to miss you so much, Nana," said Keyne.

"I will miss both of you as well," said Delia, giving Gillian a meaningful look. "You know, they're welcome to come back at any time, maybe even just for the weekend."

"That would be nice," said Gilly.

Delia reached out to touch her daughter's arm. "You could stay, too."

"I'm totally snowed in at work. I'm not sure if I could," Gilly said.

"Even in the weekends?" Delia asked. "What kind of firm are you working for?"

"A very busy one," said Gillian. "It's mostly just the stress of starting a new job. When I'm not working, I'm just recovering, you know?"

"I do know," Delia empathised. "You remember what it was like when I was involved in a big production."

"Every single time," Gillian said, her voice carrying a hint of resentment. "You'd disappear for weeks on end. I'd hardly see you unless I went to the theatre to watch rehearsals."

"I'm so sorry, love," said Delia.

"No. I understand," Gillian assured her. "Just like you should understand now. This is my career. I need to do what I need to do."

"And you're a better mother for it," said Kitty. "There is nothing worse than an unfulfilled person, you know, like people who sacrifice themselves to help others but seethe in toxic resentment for it...They probably need to be doing something creative rather than taking it out on the people around them they're so desperate to help!"

"And my work is creative," said Gilly. "I love it."

"Well, if that's your passion," said Kitty, "then you go for it!"

Merryn smiled. "Mum loves her work, but she loves us too."

"Of course she does," Delia agreed. "As do I."

"Are you going to do more theatre, Nana?" asked Keyne. "With the Myrtlewood Players?"

"You know, I think I might," said Delia. "It was fun once I got over myself."

"You've been doing local theatre?" Gillian asked in shock. "Community stuff? Heaven forbid. I thought you were far too much of a snob for that sort of thing."

"So did I," said Kitty, with a tone of amusement, "but she had a great time."

"We all did," said Merryn.

"And that's what's important," Delia said.

Gillian grinned. "Well, I have to say, I like the idea. If you do intend on staying in Myrtlewood, it might be a good idea for you...keep occupied and all that. A challenge without all the extra pressure, maybe it will be perfect."

"You know, it's funny," Delia said. "I can't even imagine going back to the West End now. It just seems so..."

"Too much like hard work?" Kitty suggested.

Delia shrugged. "Maybe my heart's just not in it anymore."

"Maybe it will be someday," Gillian said thoughtfully. "You might just need a good rest."

They finished the meal with one of Marjie's delicious lemon sponge cakes for dessert. Then it was time to say goodbye.

"We made you something special," Keyne said.

"Oh yes!" Merryn ran to the back door, returning with an envelope.

It looked to be covered in rose petals and rosemary sprigs.

"What's inside?" Delia asked, curious.

Keyne shook his head. "Oh no. You can't open it," he said. "It's not like that."

"What is it like then?" Delia asked.

"It's magic," Merryn said solemnly.

"Magic, you say?" Delia asked, intrigued. "Well then, it must be very special."

"It will protect you," Keyne explained. "We spent all day

doing a magic spell to protect our Nana from anything that might hurt her."

"So you'll be safe, Nana," Merryn assured her.

Delia smiled warmly at the children's thoughtful gesture. "How does it work?"

"Well..." Merryn and Keyne both placed their hands on the envelope. "With our love, we protect you," they chanted, their voices blending in unison.

The envelope began to glow, and Delia gasped, mortified that she might have accidentally set it on fire. But the glow had a twinkle to it. Her mouth gaped in astonishment.

"It's real magic," said Merryn.

Gillian's handbag fell to the floor as she clutched her chest in surprise. "How did you do this?"

"It's real magic, see? We are magic. Just like you, Nana," Keyne said.

Gillian's eyes were wide in shock.

Delia bit her lip. "I suppose I have some explaining to do."

27

GWYNETH

In the secluded chamber, lit only by the flickering flames of candles, Gwyneth held the black mirror with a steady hand.

The mirror's surface rippled, and soon Mathilda's image coalesced into view, her face betraying exhaustion.

"Mathilda."

"Sister Gwyneth," Mathilda replied with a respectful nod. "I have completed the task as best I could. I warned them. I offered them our help. The charms have been handed over to the crones who would take them. Agatha didn't. Ingrid did, to my surprise."

At the mention of Ingrid, a fleeting vision flashed across Gwyneth's mind: a sunlit meadow, laughter ringing in the air, two young women – hands clasped, eyes sparkling with shared secrets and dreams. She quickly shook her head, as if to dispel the ghost of a memory that dared to surface.

Gwyneth's eyes narrowed slightly. "And Ingrid? Was she cooperative?"

Mathilda hesitated, her gaze shifting briefly before meeting Gwyneth's once again. "She was reticent, as expected. Ingrid's ways have not softened with time."

Gwyneth's lips pressed into a thin line. "Reticence from Ingrid is no surprise. Her path has always been...divergent."

With a measured tone, Mathilda continued. "Perhaps you might have more luck in persuading her. Your past...connection could be influential."

"Leave the compound?" Gwyneth's voice rose with a tinge of outrage. "I have barely set foot beyond these walls since Ingrid left. She was always a...a taint on the sanctity of this place."

Gwyneth's gaze momentarily drifted to a painting on the wall, a serene landscape disrupted by a gathering storm. It mirrored a pang of longing she dared not voice.

Mathilda's expression softened, her eyes reflecting a hint of understanding. "Surely, your memories of Ingrid hold more *fondness* than that," she suggested gently.

The words hit Gwyneth like a physical blow. For a moment, her composure faltered.

Mathilda, clearly sensing the shift in the elder's demeanour, continued cautiously, "Sister Gwyneth, I understand this is difficult, but Ingrid's knowledge could be vital. Her insight..."

Gwyneth interrupted, bitterly. "Ingrid's 'insight' led her away from us, away from our teachings. She chose a different path, a path that has brought more questions than answers."

"Yet, she still holds a piece of our history," Mathilda gently prodded, her words careful, like one navigating a field of hidden thorns.

"She made her choices a long time ago."

Mathilda nodded understandingly. "But perhaps this is an opportunity for closure, for understanding. Maybe even for healing."

The word 'healing' hung in the air, hinting at old wounds not yet mended. Gwyneth let out a heavy sigh, her gaze drifting towards the mountains again.

"You speak of healing, Mathilda, but some things are beyond repair," Gwyneth whispered, more to herself than to Mathilda. "The Sisterhood requires my focus. Personal...sentiments must not cloud our purpose."

Mathilda's voice softened further. "Of course, Sister Gwyneth. I meant no disrespect. I only hoped..."

Unable to continue, Gwyneth abruptly ended the conversation; she raised a hand, a silent gesture to halt. "Your hope is not misguided, Mathilda. But the path I walk now, the path we all walk within the Sisterhood, is one of sacrifice and duty. Our personal desires must be set aside for the greater good."

There was a finality in Gwyneth's words, a closing of a door long left ajar. Mathilda bowed her head in respect, understanding the conversation had reached its end.

"Very well. I shall continue as instructed," Mathilda said,

fading from the mirror, leaving Gwyneth alone with the echoes of a past she had tried so desperately to leave behind.

As the connection severed, Gwyneth was left alone once more, the silence of her chamber enveloping her like a shroud.

The night outside whispered of a past filled with laughter and love, a past that now seemed as distant as the stars shining in the night.

She gazed out at the dark sky, punctuated by the jagged outlines of the mountains. They loomed like silent sentinels, guardians of secrets and echoes of bygone days. The night air carried whispers of a time when her world was not confined within these walls, a time when Ingrid was more than just a shadow in her heart; the exhilaration of running through the hills, the thrill of discovery, and the bond of friendship that had seemed unbreakable.

Ingrid.

They had been inseparable, two souls entwined by a shared yearning for knowledge and freedom. But choices had carved a deep crevice between their lives.

Ingrid, with her insatiable curiosity and defiant spirit, had always been too wild to be contained for long. Her departure from the Sisterhood had left a void in Gwyneth's heart, a space filled with echoes of what could have been.

As the flames danced in the hearth, casting shadows that flickered like spectres on the walls, Gwyneth's mind wandered to that fateful day. The day Ingrid had stood before her, eyes alight with a fire that threatened to consume them both, challenging the very foundations of their beliefs. The day Gwyneth had to choose.

She had chosen the path of duty and devotion to the Veiled Sisterhood. After all, it was all she knew, her entire world.

The spectre of Ingrid haunted her, still.

She turned away from the window, the mountains now mere silhouettes against the night sky. Her duty to the Sisterhood remained her guiding star, despite the shadows of the past.

28

DELIA

Gillian looked even paler as Delia talked her through the basic happenings of the past few weeks.

"So it turns out you've been a witch all this time, and I never knew," Gillian said.

"Neither did I!" said Delia. "Not until I started setting things on fire with my mind, and even then, I was in denial for a good while."

"There's a whole magical world out there," said Kitty. "Full of notorious things: werewolves, fairy creatures, vampires, shifters. It's dangerous, really!"

Gillian smiled nervously. "Uh huh. Why didn't you tell me any of this, Mum?"

"I didn't want you to institutionalise me," Delia admitted.

"Fair enough," Gillian conceded.

"And I suppose it's time I told you about your father," said Delia. "The real truth about him."

"It's not gang stuff, is it?" Gillian said. "I did think that was a bit far, even for him."

Delia sighed. "Well, it's not entirely far from the truth."

Delia began to explain, with Kitty's input, as the children embarked on one last mission around the house to make sure they hadn't forgotten anything.

"That's outrageous," said Gillian, though she didn't seem too overwhelmed by the news.

"You're taking all this rather well," Kitty remarked, patting her on the shoulder.

Gillian sighed. "It's a lot to take in. It might take me a few days to process...or a few years."

Delia smiled. "Now, are you going to finally tell me what's going on with you?"

Gillian's spine stiffened. "I need a little bit more time, Mum." she said, her voice strained.

"Is it your health? Or something else?" asked Delia, concerned.

"Please, just...give me time," Gillian replied, looking pensive. "I haven't got my head around it all. And this is so much to take in. I don't know..."

"Take the time you need, love," Delia said reassuringly. "But know that you can tell me anything."

"Gosh, especially now," Kitty said. "Delia's just revealed her biggest secret."

Gillian smiled reassuringly. Moments later, as she left with the children, Kitty and Delia stood in the doorway, waving goodbye.

"Do you think she's got some sort of magic, too?" Kitty pondered aloud.

"Don't you think she would have told me?" Delia said.

"Perhaps," Kitty said thoughtfully. "She wasn't as shocked as I thought she would be. She didn't even ask you to demonstrate your powers. That would have been the first thing I'd do."

"The first thing you did was try to seduce your captors," Delia reminded her, a playful tone in her voice.

"Not true. I did that *before* I knew you had magic," Kitty retorted.

"You're incorrigible," Delia said, shaking her head but smiling. "And I love you very much."

"I love you too, darling," said Kitty. "Now, how about a nightcap? I have a new fae wine I'm just dying to try out."

They grinned at each other.

29

THE CLERIC

The Cleric's fingers were raw, the once-pristine skin chafed and reddened by the relentless scrubbing of the Order's cold stone floors. His hands, once reserved for the manipulation of sacred texts and mystical artifacts, now clutched a coarse brush, moving back and forth in a rhythm that mirrored the monotony of his circular thoughts. The rough bristles scraped against the hard surface, each stroke a visceral reminder of his fall from grace.

As he worked, the scent of the pine soap mixed with the mustiness of the ancient hallways, creating an oppressive aroma. It was a stark contrast to the incense-laden air of his former office, where every breath was a reminder of his exalted position within the Order. Now, the simplicity of soap and water was an anchor, dragging him down into the reality of his new, humbled existence.

The repetitive motion of scrubbing, the constant pressure against his palms, was supposed to ground him in his shame, a form of physical repentance. Yet, perhaps it was achieving the opposite of this. Each circle he scrubbed into the floor was a small universe of his making, a temporary order he could impose in the violent chaos wrought by the devastating secret he now knew.

The Order of Crimson is a lie.

He paused, leaning on the brush, and gazed out of the narrow window. The world outside seemed distant, as if he were observing it from the bottom of a deep well. The sky was a dull grey, mirroring the colourless landscape of his inner world.

His traitor of a mind crept back to that ghastly chamber where he had faced what he had believed to be the divine.

The encounter sent a shiver down his spine that prickled out to his fingertips. A visceral reaction.

The darkness he had seen there was not the benevolent light of the Almighty he had been taught to revere. It was something else entirely, something so devoid of goodness that it had left him hollow.

The sense of betrayal was acute. Everything he had been taught, everything he had dedicated his life to, was now in question. The teachings of the Order, the very fabric of his belief, had unravelled before his eyes.

The Cleric's hands trembled as he resumed his scrubbing, each movement a struggle against the tide of his thoughts. The once clear and structured world of the Order had turned into a maze of deception and lies.

With each rinse of the brush, and each wring of the cloth, he felt as though he was trying to cleanse more than just the floors. He was trying to wash away the utter disillusionment, the betrayal, the fear of what really lay beyond the confines of the Order.

But the stains were stubborn, ingrained in the very stones he toiled upon, just as the stains on his soul seemed permanent, a constant reminder of his shattered faith and the dark truth he had uncovered.

In the midst of his menial labour, the Cleric was, yet again, forced to confront the most harrowing of truths: the god he had worshipped, the cause he had served, was not the beacon of righteousness he had believed it to be. And in that revelation, he found himself lost, adrift in a sea of doubt, with no shore in sight.

His hands trembled, not from the physical exertion of his new, lowly duties, but from the shattering of his once unshakeable faith.

He moved on to his next task. The broom reminded him of something...the witches. Were they really the evil temptresses set on the further moral contamination and destruction of the world he'd always been taught they were? Was that, too, a lie? Were all women not meant to be subservient? Were the Crones simply human and struggling against fate, just as he too now was?

These absurd thoughts continued to plague him as he worked.

As he swept the stone floors of the ancient hallways, his

movements were automatic, devoid of the zeal that once fuelled every action he took for the Order. The broom in his hands felt like a leaden weight, each stroke a reminder of his fall from grace. The dust he gathered seemed to mock him, a symbol of the futility of his past convictions.

In the dim light of the compound, he caught glimpses of the old tapestries that adorned the walls, once sources of inspiration, now hollow and meaningless. The depictions of a benevolent, all-powerful deity, glowing as a golden light, the Almighty he had dedicated his life to serve, now seemed like cruel jokes. The images of divine glory and righteousness were nothing but fabric and thread, empty of the sanctity he once saw in them.

Having grown up at the compound, the Cleric had long known that the Almighty was not, as new recruits often believed, the same as the god worshipped by mainstream religions. Not the Christian God, or Jewish, or Islamic. The Almighty was a deeper and far greater power, or so he'd always believed. A transcendent divine presence. The Almighty had been a great comfort to the Cleric all his life, and yet what he'd seen in that dark chamber was a far cry from what he'd ever imagined possible.

As he polished the wooden pews in the chapel, the wood's once comforting scent now filled him with revulsion. Each pew had been a silent witness to his fervent prayers, his unyielding devotion. But now, they felt like monuments to his own naivety, to the lies he had been fed and had eagerly swallowed.

He remembered the teachings he had received since childhood, the glorification of a god of all, a symbol of goodness and justice. But the reality that had been unveiled to him in that dark chamber was a betrayal of those teachings. What he had seen was not a god of light and love, but a being, or perhaps an absence of being, that exuded darkness and horror.

The more he reflected on it, the more the foundations of his belief crumbled. The structure of the Order, the hierarchy he had respected, the missions he had undertaken – all were built on a deceit so profound it was unfathomable. He realised he had been a pawn in a game he barely understood, a game where the rules were set by those who wielded power and manipulation, not by divine decree.

In the depths of his turmoil, as he tended to the most humble of tasks, the Cleric faced the most daunting question of his life: What path to take when every step leads further into darkness?

The Cleric had moved through his recent days like a ghost, his motions automatic and devoid of purpose. The once revered halls of the Order, with their high, vaulted ceilings and the quiet murmur of sacred chants, now echoed with the hollowness of his fractured soul. By day, he clung to the remnants of his sanity, performing his menial tasks with a mechanical precision that belied the turmoil churning within him.

But as night descended, the façade crumbled. In the darkness of his sparse chamber, with its austere cot and barren walls, the madness quaked within him. It was a living thing, a beast clawing at the edges of his mind, threatening to consume him. Sleep, when it came, was fitful and fleeting, a mere pause in the relentless assault of his thoughts.

He would wake, heart pounding, from nightmares too horrific to voice. The screams that tore from his throat were strangled by the oppressive silence of his room, leaving him gasping, drenched in a cold sweat. The darkness around him seemed to press in, suffocating, as if the air itself was contaminated by the evil he had glimpsed in the chamber.

The compound, once a haven of order and piety, now appeared as a grotesque parody of its former self. The stone corridors, lined with ancient tapestries depicting the Order's glorious past, felt like the insides of a mausoleum, cold and unyielding. The flickering torches cast sinister shadows that danced mockingly on the walls.

The monks, with their heads bowed in reverence and their voices lifted in prayer, seemed like marionettes, their strings pulled by an unseen, malevolent force. Where he once saw devotion and discipline, he now saw only blind obedience to a corrupt and malevolent entity.

The gardens, once a place of contemplation and peace, now appeared overgrown and wild, as if nature itself was rebelling against the Order's deceit. The once orderly rows of herbs and flowers were tangled and unkempt, mirroring the chaos that reigned in the Cleric's mind.

With each passing day, the Cleric felt himself slipping further into the abyss. The world around him, once so clear and defined, was now a blur of shadows and whispers, a labyrinth with no exit.

He glanced around the compound, at the monks scuttling here and there. Now, rather than seeing it as he once did, as picturesque order which should be brought forth into the rest of the world according to the will of the Almighty, he now saw it as a sham. An utter deception. They had all been duped into following something so sinister and terrifying that the cleric could not begin to form words to describe it.

Moment by moment, as he toiled through his punishment, he felt the break inside himself widen, until he was nothing, until there was nothing – nothing left, but madness.

30

DELIA

Delia rose early. She had already packed her bags the day before, but after fretting in the night, she decided to re-pack. Obviously she needed warm clothes, but what else. She couldn't carry too much with her for the 'adventure' – as Marjie had so optimistically called it. She was at a loss. Other than the basics, what else items could she bring that would be truly useful?

The aroma of coffee wafted up from the kitchen, luring her downstairs.

Delia made her way down to see Kitty in the kitchen, pouring a cup. She handed it over to Delia with an unimpressed smile.

"You're up early," said Delia.

"I couldn't sleep," Kitty admitted. "I was too worried about you going off with those other old biddies. Do you really have to go? It's so dangerous...and leaving me here all alone."

"You're old enough to take care of yourself, surely!"

Kitty sighed and Delia hugged her.

"Why don't you go and stay with Ursula again?" Delia suggested. "She and Ashwyn would love the company, and you're great with the children."

"Maybe I will." Kitty shrugged. "But I still don't like the idea of you going, though."

"I know. I'm not sure I want to go either. But I feel I must. I'm committed now, aren't I?"

"You could uncommit," suggested Kitty weakly, sipping her coffee. "Oh, who am I kidding. I can't stop you. You're going to do what you're going to do, regardless of the risks. I just wish I had some way of helping."

Delia smiled. "Knowing that you care about me is help enough."

She gave Kitty another reassuring hug, nearly spilling their coffee in the process.

They shared a quick breakfast of eggs and toast, while Torin begged for crusts under the table.

"Now, you're going to stay with Kitty and look after her," Delia instructed Torin.

Her familiar whined a little, and pawed at the ground.

"I'm serious," Delia added. "I need you to do a good job protecting my most important friend while I'm away."

It was true, she wanted Kitty to have the company, and not

to mention she didn't want to risk the pup's life, considering the danger she was about to throw herself into once again. Myrtlewood was safe enough, but wherever they were going was bound to be outside its protective field.

As Delia went to leave, Kitty cleared her throat. "Aren't you forgetting something?"

"Another hug?" Delia asked.

"No." Kitty gestured to the table where the special envelope gifted to Delia by her grandchildren still sat. "Take that with you. It's for your protection, you know."

A warm smile graced Delia's face. "It's funny. This morning, I was fretting about what useful things I could take. And yet, it seems my grandchildren have already provided something. I wonder what it will actually do...whether it will help."

Kitty, with a touch of pride, noted, "It's certainly magical... even as non-magical as I might be." She huffed.

"Oh darling," said Delia. "I'm sorry this whole thing has been tough on you."

"In a way," Kitty said dismissively. "But actually, I've enjoyed all the time with you and the little ones. They are delightful. Don't get me wrong. I'm glad I never had children of my own, I couldn't bear the responsibility. But I do love spending time with them, especially your grandkids – they're both little witches."

"Don't remind me," said Delia. "I've enough to be worrying about right at this moment."

"Well, maybe their magic will help you." Kitty picked up the envelope, handing it to Delia who slid it into her inner coat pocket, enjoying the warmth that radiated from the gift.

This reassured Delia. Despite stepping into the unknown, she was loved and protected.

31

MARJIE

Marjie made her way through the lush embrace of the forest towards Ingrid's house, with Delia and Agatha at her side. She inhaled the air, rich with the earthy scent of moss, and enjoyed the chorus of birdsong as if it were a choir. The forest floor was covered with leaves which softened their steps, while beams of sunlight streaked through the foliage, casting dappled patterns over them. Marjie's heightened emotions had been overwhelming, recently, but here in nature, she relaxed, as the forest eased the burdens of her heart.

She turned to Agatha, refreshed and ready for banter. "You're wearing a smile today," Marjie said. "Have you finally learned to conjure one, or is it just the forest playing tricks on my eyes?"

Agatha, with the timing and precision of a seasoned spell caster, parried effortlessly. "Oh, Marjie, if only I could conjure patience to endure your humour. Alas, some realms of magic remain elusive."

Marjie chuckled, feeling a wave of affection for her old friend. Agatha's mood was indeed lighter today, a welcome change, particularly in Delia's presence.

Perhaps these old woods have worked their magic on her too, Marjie mused, glancing at Agatha with curiosity. *Though her grumpiness had eased a little by the time we left Delia's house.*

One of the side-effects of her burgeoning powers of empathy was that Marjie knew far more about the people around her than she actually wanted to. She could tell that Covvey had something to do with Agatha's recent foul mood, just as she could tell that Delia harboured rather more than burning rage and resentment for that rogue tracker she'd cast out of the pub. It didn't pay to raise these kinds of things, though; in Marjie's experience they were best left on the back burner to simmer away until the time came when people were ready to confront them.

She glanced across to Delia who'd been awfully quiet, as if deep in thought. Considering that it was best not to disturb her, Marjie nudged Agatha playfully. "I do believe the trees have softened your edges, Agatha. Or is it that age has finally brought wisdom?"

Agatha's laugh, a rare and delightful sound, echoed through the trees. "Marjie, dear, if wisdom comes with age, then there's no hope for any of us, is there?"

Their laughter melded with the rustling leaves.

As they approached Ingrid's home, Marjie felt a familiar

surge of anticipation. It wasn't too long ago that she'd never seen the inside of the hut, and she'd been terrified of the forest witch, but now they were fast becoming old friends.

As the group approached Ingrid's cottage, they found her in the midst of a comical yet earnest negotiation with the dragon, stubbornly in its puppy form. The creature, with an obstinate glint in its eyes, seemed to be enjoying the challenge of being coaxed into the goat cart.

Marjie, still chuckling from her exchange with Agatha, couldn't help but smile at the sight. "Seems we've arrived just in time for the daily dragon drama."

"If you won't get in, we'll leave you behind," Agatha warned the puppy, climbing into the cart and taking a seat. She looked over to the other crones. "That goes for you lot, too. What are you waiting for? We have a mission, don't we?"

Agatha smirked. "Can't we just ride the dragon?"

Ingrid, hands on her hips, glared at Agatha sternly. "Dragons aren't horses, Agatha. I'd like to see you try to drive one, you foolish woman."

Delia, standing slightly apart, watched the interaction with a bemused expression, clearly entertained by the dynamics of her fellow Crones.

The dragon puppy, perhaps realising it was the centre of attention, made a show of indecision before finally, with a dramatic huff, leaping into the cart. It clambered directly onto Ingrid's knee.

Ingrid looked down at the dragon now comfortably nestled in her lap. "I can't very well drive like this, now can I?"

Agatha, climbing into the cart, added, "Or perhaps the dragon prefers to be the co-pilot today."

Marjie and Delia followed her.

Ingrid, finally managing to gently shift the dragon to a more suitable spot beside her, chuckled. "Welcome to a typical day in our lives, where dragons are puppies, and nothing is quite as it seems."

With the dragon settled, the goats bleated and the cart began to move, pulling them swiftly along the narrow path leading out of the forest.

Marjie, seizing the moment of calm, retrieved her knitting from a small bag. The rhythmic clickety-clack of her needles began to accompany the steady trot of the goat cart, adding a homely, familiar sound to the tranquillity of the forest.

"Do we even know where we're going?" Agatha asked abruptly.

Ingrid, guiding the goat cart with practiced ease, turned to glare at her. "I'll have you know that I've figured out our destination, as much as one can with these old maps and cryptic clues." She paused, her gaze thoughtful. "If my intuition and the book are right, the elder grove is not too far from here, rather near to where I grew up."

At Ingrid's words, the cart, enchanted with spells for swiftness, began to pick up pace. The landscape subtly shifted as they neared the edge of the forest, entering a realm of frosty moors, fields, and meadows.

Delia looked out at the expansive open space. "It's so eerily quiet here, so different from when we last left Ingrid's house by goat cart. No pursuit, no urgency. Just this...stillness. It would be relaxing if it wasn't so eerie."

Indeed, the moors, covered in a thin layer of frost and the openness of the landscape, lent an air of vulnerability, yet there was beauty in its starkness.

Marjie felt a slight shiver, not from cold, but from the realisation of how far they had come, both in distance and in their lives in just a few short weeks. "I agree. It's peaceful, yes," she mused aloud, "but one can never be too cautious. The quiet has its own secrets, after all."

As the goat cart continued its journey, the crones settled into a companionable silence, each lost in their thoughts, yet united in their purpose.

Marjie wrapped her shawl tighter around her shoulders, a shiver running down her spine. The eerie stillness of the landscape, so different from the sheltered forest they had left behind, seemed to resonate with a quiet intensity. She could sense the emotions of her fellow Crones, both relief and underlying tension.

Marjie cast furtive glances towards Delia. Something was different about her today, but she couldn't put her finger on what it was.

Agatha, her eyes scanning the horizon, interjected with her characteristic pragmatism. "Don't get too comfortable. Once we're beyond Myrtlewood's protective cloak, we're fair game again. The Order's tracker is no amateur; we'd do well to remember that."

The mention of the Order, and especially the tracker,

seemed to ignite a spark in Delia. Her emotions flared so strongly that Marjie could actually see them, a sure sign of her burgeoning powers responding to the perceived threat. The air around her crackled with energy, her fiery nature barely contained beneath the surface.

"Settle down," Agatha scolded, her tone firm yet not unkind. "We can't have you setting us all on fire."

Marjie watched Delia take a deep breath, visibly trying to rein in her emotions.

Marjie glanced at Ingrid, who navigated the cart with a steady hand, her gaze fixed on the path ahead.

The goat cart ambled onto a narrow bridge spanning a small river, its wooden planks creaking under the weight. As they reached the midpoint, Marjie noticed the water below beginning to ripple and swirl in unusual patterns. It wasn't the wind or the movement of the cart, but something else – an unseen force emanating from her.

Agatha, observing the phenomenon, turned to Marjie with a raised eyebrow. "That's your power then?"

Marjie sighed. "I'm afraid so," she admitted. "It's been a bit unruly lately. I can barely make a pot of tea without causing a fuss in the teashop. I've had to rely on Papa Jack to cover for me, but that's hardly a solution." Her hands worked her knitting needles more frantically, betraying her inner turmoil.

Gazing out at the flowing river, Marjie's thoughts drifted to Papa Jack. He was a dear friend, of course. His warmth, his understanding, his mere presence had a way of calming the turbulence within her. She missed him when he wasn't around, yet she harboured doubts about growing closer to him. She had to protect her heart, especially as it was currently overflowing with feeling.

The cart moved on, into the open wilderness, as they neared the mountains. Marjie peered up at them, their jagged edges foreboding. Not for the first time, she wondered what on earth they were getting themselves into.

32

INGRID

The near-setting sun cast soft golden light over the rocky terrain. Ingrid guided the goat cart along a narrow, winding path. The looming mountainside, with its formidable presence, stirred a sense of nostalgia within her.

A faint, cool breeze carried the scent of mountain herbs crushed under the cart's wheels.

Ingrid glanced over her shoulder at the crones in the back, noting the dragon puppy nestled comfortably among them. "Not far to go now."

The familiar, rugged landscape evoked memories of her rebellious youth, of days spent exploring these very mountains with Gwyneth by her side. Those hours of stolen freedom and daring were a stark contrast to the disciplined life under the watchful eyes of the sisterhood.

Trying to push away the bittersweet memories, Ingrid

focused on the path ahead, but the whisper of the past was persistent. The mountain seemed to echo with laughter from a time long gone.

"There's hardly any snow until further up the mountain," Ingrid muttered. "It's just as well we haven't had snowfall for days."

"And hopefully not for a few days more at that," Agatha added. "It has been an unusually snowy winter, aside from those summery days that your dearest ones brought about, Marjie."

Marjie glared at Agatha. "It wasn't Rosemary and Athena's fault, you know that. But yes, it has been a rather snowy winter overall. I wonder whether it's the seasons re-balancing themselves or whether it's us."

"Us?" Agatha said sharply. "What do we have to do with any of it?"

"You know," Marjie said, her knitting needles continuing to click rhythmically. "Winter is the season of the crone and all that – maybe our rising powers are making the season stronger."

As the goat cart snaked its way along the mountain path, Marjie and Agatha traded playful insults which largely revolved around comparing each other to goats.

Delia sat quietly as if lost in her own thoughts. Ingrid sensed her apprehension, but her focus remained fixed on navigating the terrain.

She thought of Mathilda, wondering where she might be now. Was she still in Myrtlewood, or had she returned to the safe gilded cage of the compound? Even as a child, Ingrid had longed for the freedom of these mountains, the open skies, and the untamed wilderness.

Now, as the evening light draped the landscape, Ingrid reached for her trusty monocle. This was no ordinary glass; it was a tool of vision, extending her sight far beyond the ordinary. Bringing it to her eye, she scanned the horizon. The crones leaned forward in anticipation, their earlier banter giving way to a shared sense of purpose.

"There it is." Ingrid's voice was sharp with excitement as she spotted their destination. Through the lens, a vibrant patch of green stood out starkly against the icy grey of the mountain rock face. "Evergreen, and unlike ordinary elders in many other ways..."

The grove, shrouded in mystery and ancient magic, beckoned them closer.

"Strange that it's still standing after all these years of legend," Agatha muttered. "Leave it to Ingrid to find a grove that's as stubborn and enduring as she is."

Marjie chuckled. "And just as hidden and full of secrets, no doubt."

The air seemed to thrum with energy as they drew nearer. Ingrid steered them forward towards this place of power, where the old ways whispered their secrets to those who dared to listen.

33
AGATHA

Agatha let out a soft sigh as the goat cart rolled into the elder grove mountainside, and the scene transformed dramatically. The space opened out like a parliament of watchful wise trees, centred around a glimmering clearing. These were no ordinary elders, like the flimsy deciduous bushes in her back garden or even the gnarled old tree in Ingrid's. These enormous trees, lush and vibrant, reached towards the sky, their leaves glinting in the sunlight, casting a majestic and ethereal glow over the area.

Agatha, usually so contained and stoic, experienced an uncharacteristic wave of transcendent joy. The sheer beauty of the grove seemed to lift her spirit, infusing her with a sense of optimism that rivalled even Marjie's usual buoyancy.

"For the first time in ages, I don't miss my library," Agatha mused aloud, a rare admission that drew a surprised glance from Marjie. The grove's resplendent beauty held the attention of Agatha's usually wandering mind. Her cherished sanctuary of books and solitude, which had always been her escape, now paled in comparison to what was before her.

Marjie, seizing the moment for a light-hearted jab, quipped, "Who are you, and what have you done with Agatha? I never thought I'd see the day when you'd prefer nature over your dusty old tomes."

Agatha shot back, her eyes twinkling with humour, "Oh, shush, Marjie. Even I am allowed my moments of awe. Don't make me regret sharing them."

They disembarked from the cart, and the dragon puppy, sensing the change in environment, scampered around with renewed energy, its playful antics bringing smiles to their faces.

The divine presence of the grove, its power and beauty defied all logic and reason.

The crones moved through the grove, each step taking them deeper into its enchanting heart. The air was alive with the whispers of ancient trees and the secrets they held.

Agatha felt a profound sense of peace, a rare feeling that she cherished.

"Ahh," said Ingrid. "See here, there's a sign."

She gestured to an old stone plinth with letters etched in gold.

"The Grove of Elders Blaze," Delia read. "So that's the official name of this amazing place. I wonder how many people have ever discovered it all the way out here."

"Not many, I'd wager," said Ingrid. "These mountains are

concealed to mundane eyes. It looks like only moors in this direction from the roads."

"What secrets are being hidden under all that magic?" Delia asked. "But I can't complain. This place would surely be a mess if the tourists all knew about it!"

Each crone reacted differently to the grove's allure. Delia had a look of quiet reverence in her eyes as she gently brushed her fingers against the bark of an elder. Marjie, ever the spirited one, twirled around, her laughter mingling with the soft rustle of leaves, as if the grove itself rejoiced in her joy. Ingrid stood in awed silence, taking in every detail. Agatha watched them, a rare smile playing on her lips. Here, away from the confines of the familiar, they were free to be their truest selves.

Agatha stepped deeper into the Elders Blaze grove, enveloped in the atmosphere of its ancient mystique. The trees reaching so high above they seemed to soar. On closer inspection, each seemed to emit a faint, ethereal glow not just from the sunlight, but from within, as if holding the very essence of the grove's magic. Agatha found herself lost in wonder at the sight, her usual reserve melting away under the grove's spell.

The breeze here was a gentle entity, whispering through the leaves and branches, carrying with it the soft murmurs of the forest as though it were speaking directly to her, a song of the ages that resonated deep within her soul. She closed her eyes for a moment, allowing the melody to wash over her, feeling a connection to the grove that was both ancient and immediate.

Opening her eyes again, Agatha was captivated by the sunbeams filtering through the canopy. The ground, blanketed with lush moss and fallen leaves, released an earthy fragrance with each step she took, grounding her in the moment.

Around her, the grove was alive with subtle movements; wildflowers in pockets of sunlight glowed as if lit from within, their colours vibrant against the deep greens of the grove. The air was filled with their sweet scent, adding to the ethereal quality of the place. It was as if the grove itself was in a state of gentle celebration, rejoicing in its own secluded beauty.

Lost in the moment, Agatha felt a rare sense of peace, a tranquillity that was new to her. Here, Agatha felt a part of something larger, something eternal.

As the dragon puppy scampered around, her playful antics seemed to personify the grove's spirit. Agatha observed the creature with a newfound curiosity, ancient yet childlike. It was as if the grove awakened a part of her essence previously unseen, revealing the depth of magic it possessed.

Ingrid ran her fingers over the moss-covered rocks, feeling the pulse of the earth beneath. Her powers clearly resonated with the grove's energy, as steady as the earth itself.

Marjie reached into her handbag and produced a small box. "Time for a pot of tea!"

Delia laughed. "Trust you to think of tea even amongst all this majestic beauty."

"There's always time for tea," Marjie insisted.

Agatha cackled with the other crones.

The grove, in all its glory, seemed to hold the answers to questions they hadn't yet asked. Agatha knew that the tranquillity of this moment was a precious respite. Challenges lay ahead, hidden in the shadows of the ancient trees. But for now, they were content to be in the presence of the grove's divine beauty, united in their quest and strengthened.

34

THE SHEPHERD

In the dimly lit confines of his quarters, Father Benedict moved with a purpose that had long been brewing in the depths of his being. The Elders of the Order of Crimson had denied his requests too many times, their conservative approach a shackle to his ambitions, and furthermore, it was an insult, not only to his tireless efforts, but to his intellect. Tonight, he would break those chains.

The room was filled with relics of his long service to the Order, each artifact a token of his dedication. He paused, his hand lingering over an old, leather-bound tome, its pages filled with forbidden knowledge that he had secretly studied over the years. The flickering candlelight cast long, dancing shadows across the walls, mirroring the tumultuous thoughts swirling in his mind.

Tonight, the course of the Order changes, and with it, the fate of those who dare stand in my way.

He gazed at the map spread out on his desk, his finger tracing the route the tracker would take.

This time, that rogue would serve a purpose far beyond mere surveillance. Father Benedict had made his expectations clear, his threats leaving no room for ambiguity.

The Cleric had been too lenient, too soft in his handling of the tracker.

The Shepherd would not make the same mistake.

He'd wanted the Crones alive in order to steal their power, but now that a far greater power was within his grasp, perhaps a new strategy was required.

The clock struck midnight, its chimes resonating through the silent quarters. Father Benedict rose, his movements deliberate, his heart tight with anticipation and resolve. He donned his cloak, its fabric whispering along the stone floor as he made his way out.

Each step Benedict took resonated against the ancient stones, a solitary sound in the otherwise silent passage. He felt the eyes of the past upon him, the long-gone members of the Order who had walked these same paths. Their whispers seemed to linger in the air, a ghostly chorus to his solitary march. *Their time has passed. It is my turn to shape our destiny.*

The underground corridors of the compound were eerily silent, save for the occasional drip of water from the ancient stone ceilings. The guards, stationed at the entrance to the inner sanctum, lounged against the wall, revealing their appalling lack of discipline.

"Stand up straight," he instructed.

The guards righted their posture quickly, fear flashing in their eyes.

Father Benedict scrutinised them, noting every crease in their uniforms, every sign of neglect. "You represent the Order," he hissed, his voice low but fierce. "Your appearance should be as impeccable as your duty. Anything less is an affront to the Almighty we serve." The guards shifted uncomfortably.

"My apologies, sir," said the shorter guard. "It won't happen again."

Father Benedict's gaze hardened. "This is out of order! Your collars are scuffed and your shirts un-ironed," he scolded them. "You disgrace the Order with such sloppiness. Go and right yourselves immediately."

The guards protested weakly, "But sir, we cannot leave our post..."

Benedict cut them off with a wave of his hand, authority radiating from his very being. "This is not a suggestion. It is a command. I will watch over the door. Go, now!"

Reluctantly, the guards departed, leaving Father Benedict alone. A thrill of excitement and glee coursed through him as he opened the heavy wooden door, closing it behind him with a definitive click.

The room was dark with no torchlight to illuminate it, but Benedict needed no light to find his way. The sanctum was a place few had the privilege to enter. His heart raced with over-powering reverence. Now, this sacred space was the stage for his audacious plan. He moved towards the far side, his mind awash with memories of the day, years ago, when he, a rebellious and spirited boy, was first brought to witness the Almighty. That moment had irrevocably altered the course of his life.

His hands were steady now, the initial tremble replaced by a surge of adrenaline. He could almost hear the heartbeat of the Order itself, pulsing through the walls of the chamber. This was more than a door; it was a gateway to unimaginable power, a power that had been hoarded and hidden away by the Elders. *No longer*, he vowed silently. *From now on it will be mine to wield.*

Standing before the sacred engraved door, his hands trembled slightly as he loosened the lock. The door creaked open.

Father Benedict inhaled sharply and stumbled back with the awe of one gazing upon a thousand clear night skies, its vastness unfathomable, its power beyond human comprehension. Before him lay the greatest power of the Almighty, a sight so formidable that words paled in comparison.

In that moment, Father Benedict stood on the precipice of destiny; the magnitude of what lay before him was as exhilarating as it was daunting. This was the moment he had been waiting for, the moment when he would seize the power that the Elders had so foolishly underestimated.

Father Benedict stood, trembling, before the Almighty; the air around him seemed to thrum with power. The entity before him was more than a mere physical presence; it was an overwhelming force that seemed to resonate with the very fabric of existence. The room, once shadowed, was now bathed in an ethereal light that emanated from the source of the power.

For a moment, Benedict was struck dumb, his plans and ambitions dwarfed by the sheer magnitude of what he beheld. The Almighty wasn't just a figure of worship or a symbol of the Order's faith; it was a living, breathing manifestation of power, ancient and incomprehensible. The air was electric, charged with an energy that beckoned him, called to the core of his being.

"This is it," Benedict whispered to himself, his voice barely audible over the hum of energy. "This is what I've been waiting for my entire life."

He stepped forward, terror washing over him. Here, in the presence of such power, his lifetime of service, his frustrations with the Elders, his ambitious plans – all seemed insignificant. He was in the presence of something far greater than himself, far greater than anything he had ever known.

With a deep, reverential breath, Benedict knelt before the Almighty. It was an act of submission, but also one of communion. He felt the power around him, a vast, inexhaustible well of energy, and he opened himself to it. It was as if he were a vessel, and the Almighty's power the liquid light that filled him.

The sensation was indescribable. Magic coursed through him, not just filling him, but transforming him. It was as if he were being remade from within, his very essence altered by the Almighty's energy. His mind expanded, his senses heightened, and he felt a connection to something far beyond the physical realm.

As the overwhelming power of the Almighty surged through Father Benedict, a terrifying realisation dawned upon him. This force, vast and unbridled, was not just a font of power to be harnessed – it was a storm of darkness, threatening to consume him. The energy that had initially filled him with a sense of omnipotence now roared within him like an inferno, its intensity far beyond his human capacity to contain.

Panic clawed at his heart as he grappled with the very real possibility of his own annihilation.

His body trembled uncontrollably, a mere vessel in the throes of a power it was never made to hold. Visions of his own doom flashed before his eyes – a man consumed by his own hubris, destroyed by the force he sought to control. In that harrowing moment, Benedict faced not only the potential destruction of his physical being but also the shattering of his lifelong convictions. The fear of his impending demise was a sharp, cold blade against the fervour of his ambitions, a stark reminder of the fine line between divine power and mortal folly.

The world around him blurred and warped as if the walls had melted away into nothingness and the ground beneath his feet dissolved into the void. The light that had once seemed ethereal and inviting now flared into an unbearable brilliance, searing his eyes, piercing his very soul.

Benedict's breaths came in ragged gasps, his mind reeling under the assault of the uncontainable power. He tried to cry out, to call for help, but his voice was lost in the tumultuous roar that filled his ears. His thoughts were now scattered fragments in the roar of energy that raged within him.

And then, as suddenly as it had begun, everything went black. The immense light, the deafening noise, the excruciating pain – all of it ceased in an instant, leaving Benedict in a void of absolute darkness and silence. He felt as if he were floating, weightless, in an endless expanse of nothingness.

Time seemed to lose all meaning. Benedict could not tell if seconds or hours had passed. The fears and ambitions that had driven him here seemed distant, like echoes from another life, his consciousness drifting in the vast, empty space.

In the absence of all sensory input, Father Benedict was confronted with the essence of his own being – stripped of his ambitions, his pride, his identity as a member of the Order. He faced the raw, unadorned truth of himself. He was nothing.

In this place of darkness and silence, Benedict began to understand the true nature of the power he had sought to wield. It was not a tool to be controlled or a weapon to be used for personal gain. It was a force far beyond human comprehension.

As Father Benedict slowly came to, he found himself sprawled on the cold floor of the chamber, panting heavily, his robes drenched in sweat. He lay there for a moment, disoriented, trying to piece together the fragments of his consciousness shattered by the Almighty's power. His body ached as if he had been through a great battle, every muscle tense and sore.

In the wake of that destruction, however, something new

had been born. As he slowly pushed himself up to a sitting position, a sense of clarity began to emerge from the chaos of his experience. The power of the Almighty was coursing through him.

He heard the sound of footsteps approaching. The guards, returning to their post, would soon discover him here. A sense of urgency gripped him.

He rose to his feet with a gleam in his eye.

35
DELIA

As dusk gently draped the Elders Blaze grove, Delia raised an eyebrow as Marjie held up a blue, white, and pink striped teapot.

Delia shook her head. "You're obsessed. We've already had tea."

"Stand back, everyone!" Marjie announced with a flourish.

The other Crones stepped back, their eyes fixed on the teapot in Marjie's hands. She placed it down carefully in the centre of the clearing, stepped away, and with a mischievous wink, began to chant softly.

Her words wove through the air in a delicate spell. The teapot started to quiver.

Delia's mouth fell open in awe as the small object expanded. The transformation was like watching a flower bloom in fast-forward – graceful and mesmerising. It was no longer anything resembling a teapot at all, unfolding into a large, spacious tent.

The tent's fabric was a beautiful array of pink, blue, and white stripes. It seemed to glow softly, exuding a warmth and welcome.

Delia, still in awe, hesitated at the entrance at Marjie's urging. "Go on, take a look," Marjie encouraged with a proud smile.

Stepping inside, Delia was greeted by an interior that made her mind boggle. The puppy raced around, leading the way through the tent which was divided into four separate bedrooms, each adorned with plush bedding and soft, inviting lighting. The living area was spacious and cosy, furnished with comfortable sofas and charming décor that gave it a homely feel.

But what truly took her breath away was the kitchen. It was fully equipped, boasting modern appliances that gleamed under the tent's enchanted light, alongside cabinets and a dining area that could comfortably seat all of them.

"Oh, Marjie!" Delia said, somewhat breathless. "This is more than just a tent; it's a marvel of magical engineering with the luxury of a high-end home!"

Marjie beamed, clearly pleased. "Well, we Crones deserve a bit of comfort on our adventures, don't we?"

The group settled into the tent as Marjie prepared a supper of roast vegetable soup that was both delicious and comforting. The aroma of the hearty herbs and spices filled the tent.

The warmth of the tent contrasted with the cool evening air

outside. The soft glow of lanterns cast a gentle light, and the rustling of the trees seemed like a distant lullaby. Delia savoured each bite of the meal, the flavours bursting in her mouth like a music.

"This is wonderful, Marjie," Delia said, her voice warm with gratitude.

"Not bad," Agatha added.

"That's high praise from a grumpy toad like you," Marjie jibed with a chuckle as they continued their meal.

Outside, the grove stood tall and majestic, while the tent was a delightful retreat. Sitting there with her new friends, Delia felt a sense of belonging and peace, but as the evening wore on, her calm was eroded by growing irritation, a prickling sensation that seemed to crawl up her spine.

The cosy ambiance of the tent contrasted sharply with the turmoil brewing within her. Sharp thoughts and feelings began to stab at her mind that could not be explained away by mere tiredness.

Her mind kept returning to her role in all of this, and the secrets buried somewhere in her heritage. She knew so little about it. Her grandmother, Etty, had been so prominent in Delia's early years, and yet had never revealed that she was a witch. Delia had grown up ignorant of the entire magical world. And what of Etty's death? There were too many unsolved clues, too much yet unknown and the turmoil built up to the point where she was unable to contain it any longer.

"All these mysteries are beginning to get on my nerves," Delia said. "You know, I came here for a holiday, and I suppose I was chasing the memory of my grandmother, Etty, too. But even she left me with so many unresolved questions...I wish I knew what really happened to her."

The others fell silent, turning their attention to her. It was Ingrid who responded, her tone matter-of-fact. "Your grandmother was murdered, Delia. She couldn't have possibly died in a fire like that. It just doesn't add up."

"A fire?" Delia asked, recalling vaguely that Ferg, the mayor, had mentioned fire in relation to Etty. Delia had assumed he'd been referring to her magic, not her demise. "I was told she died of emphysema!"

Agatha chuckled. "Oh no – it was supposedly a house fire. I remember everyone talking about it when I was younger. No one believed a powerful fire witch would burn up like that."

Delia leaned back in a jolt of shock, her eyes widening. There had been vague suggestions before that Etty's death had not been as simple as she'd been told as a child. "You knew?" she looked around at her supposed friends. "All of you? And you never told me?"

"I don't think I knew," Marjie muttered. "Perhaps it was before my time."

Delia's gaze fixed on Ingrid. "When we first met, I was sure there was something you weren't telling me about Etty. Why didn't you tell me?"

Agatha took a long gulp of sherry.

Ingrid, meeting Delia's gaze, replied calmly, "I didn't know anything for certain, all I had was some mild speculation based on logic and rumours...I didn't want to alarm you, especially with everything else we have on our plate. Besides, when we first met you were a right mess – out there in the woods, hiding in a hollow of tree roots. It didn't seem like the right time to dig up the past."

Delia's frustration boiled over. "So, you thought it best to keep me in the dark? Treat me like a child?" The air around her began to crackle with her rising power, the temperature in the tent rising perceptibly.

"Something's wrong," Marjie said. "We were all calm a moment ago, but now the air is loaded with tension. It's like pins all around us, stabbing at us. Can't you feel it, Delia? You're not yourself."

Delia's rage bubbled over. "I'm sick and tired of people telling me who or what I am!"

Marjie, sensing the imminent danger, waved her hand over her teacup, and the liquid from it, along with other beverages nearby, rose into the air.

"Hey, watch it!" Agatha grumbled. "What have you done with my sherry, you meddling imbecile?"

Marjie ignored her, all her attention directed at Delia, who at that moment felt the tickling of flames as the burst from her shoulders right down to her fingertips.

"Easy now," Marjie said soothingly as she directed the liquid towards Delia, dousing the flare of her powers.

Delia, dampened both physically and emotionally, glared at Ingrid. "I'm not some naïve child, Ingrid. I have a right to know about my own family."

Ingrid, her expression softening, reached out a hand, but

Delia recoiled. "I understand you're upset, Delia. I thought I was protecting you," Ingrid explained, her voice laced with regret.

Feeling suffocated and patronised, Delia stood up abruptly. "I need some air," she declared, her tone final as she stormed out of the tent, leaving the others in silence.

Outside, the grove seemed to sense her turmoil. A mist began to creep along the ground, enveloping her as she walked away, her mind a blizzard of unanswered questions while the bitterness of betrayal clung to her like a heavy cloak.

Her footsteps were muffled by the thick carpet of moss underfoot, and the grove around her began to change as the strange mist, ethereal and creeping, snaked its way across the ground, enveloping the bases of the trees and obscuring her path.

Suddenly, the ancient elder trees around her burst into flames. The fire was not of a natural kind; it was spectral, flickering in hues of blue and green, casting a surreal glow on the grove. Delia stopped in her tracks, her heart pounding. The flames didn't consume or char the trees but faded around them.

Panic set in as Delia realised she could no longer see the path back to the tent. The majestic grove was now a labyrinth of flames and swirling mist. Every direction looked the same, a reflection of her fraught mind.

Delia's breathing quickened as she spun around, trying to find a landmark, anything familiar to guide her back. But the mist thickened with her growing fear, and the flames twisted, blurring the line between reality and illusion. She was lost, not just physically, but emotionally, in the labyrinth of her thoughts.

The phantom flames leapt with menacing intent, as if drawing fuel from Delia's fears. Their crackling seemed to whisper her deepest terror with every snap and pop.

Delia's breaths came in sharp gasps. With every step, the fire painted an ever-more vivid picture of her fears. She saw visions of her grandmother's face contorted in the confusion of her final moments, the smouldering embers of her family history, the charred remnants of her own peace of mind. The flames mocked her.

In this moment, the grove was no longer a refuge but a stage for her innermost fears to play out their cruel drama. Delia knew she could not run from the fire, for it was not the grove that burned – it was her own spirit. The flames would not be quenched until she faced them.

36
INGRID

Ingrid looked around at the startled expressions of her fellow Crones. The atmosphere hung heavy in the tent after Delia's abrupt departure. The dragon puppy was curled in the corner, but her ears twitched.

Marjie started to rise from her seat. "I'll go after her."

"No," Agatha's voice cut through, commanding and firm. "Give her time to cool off."

Ingrid nodded, her hands resting in her lap, fingers intertwined. "She needs time." She understood the intensity of emotions Delia was navigating – her need for solitude, for space to untangle the threads of confusion and old pain.

"Perhaps we all need time," Ingrid added.

As the words left her lips, a strange mist began to seep into the tent, the silent flood transforming the space from a cosy sanctuary into something unsettling.

Ingrid stood up, her instincts and deep connection to the earth sensing a deeper shift.

The tent and the grove around her dissolved into the mist.

Ingrid found herself standing on a precipice, the ground beneath her feet unsteady.

The earth trembled, and she steadied herself.

There was a snarl from behind her. Ingrid's heart pounded as she turned to meet the gaze of the dragon.

Gone was the playful puppy that had frolicked around their feet; before her stood an enormous creature, far bigger than Ingrid has seen her before, even as a dragon, scales glinting in the misty light.

Ancient eyes bore into Ingrid's, a fury in their depths that was both frightening and mesmerising.

The dragon's jaws gaped open, revealing rows of sharp, gleaming teeth.

Ingrid, whose life had been full of confronting fears and embracing the strength of the earth, stood her ground.

Despite the fear that clawed at her insides, her stance was resolute. This was not just a test of her courage; it was a confrontation with the primal force of nature, a force she had devoted her life to understanding and respecting.

The ground continued to shake. Ingrid knew this was no ordinary quake.

Ingrid's heart hammered against her ribs as the ground beneath her trembled with growing ferocity. She could feel the deep, resonant vibrations of the earth's unrest as fissures began to snake across the cliff's surface. Dust and small stones cascaded down the cliff face.

The dragon, now a beast of mythic proportions, let out a thunderous roar that echoed across the expanse. Her eyes, pools of molten rage, locked onto Ingrid with a predatory stare. The creature's massive body coiled with a power that made the air itself shudder.

Ingrid's breaths were sharp and quick as she steadied her stance, preparing for the onslaught.

She had faced many perils, but none as terrifying as the one that loomed before her now. The dragon's jaws opened wider, her dagger-like teeth promising destruction.

Without warning, the cliff gave a violent lurch.

A deafening crack split the air as the earth tore wide open.

Ingrid stumbled, her well-honed balance challenged by the violent upheaval. She threw her arms out, seeking equilibrium, as the ground fell away into the abyss leaving Ingrid with precious little earth to stand on.

The dragon unfurled her gargantuan wings with a sound like the clap of thunder. She reared up onto her powerful haunches launching her immense body into the air.

Adrenaline surged through Ingrid's veins. She dodged to the side as the dragon's talons scraped the spot where she had stood a heartbeat earlier, sending showers of rock and debris into the air.

The creature's tail whipped around, a deadly appendage that Ingrid narrowly avoided with an instinctual dive.

Scrambling to her feet, Ingrid searched for any advantage,

her mind racing. She could not outmuscle the dragon, but perhaps she could outmanoeuvre her.

As the dragon circled back for another pass, Ingrid took a deep breath, calling upon her deep connection with the earth for guidance and strength.

With the dragon bearing down on her once more, Ingrid made her move. She leapt as the cliff crumbled beneath her, propelling herself towards a newly formed outcrop. She landed just as the dragon's jaw snapped shut behind her, missing her by mere inches.

Ingrid stood on the edge of the abyss with nowhere left to stand, the roar of the dragon filling her ears. There had to be another way...

37

MARJIE

The mist surged into the tent, swallowing up the warm, comfortable space. Marjie, caught off guard, watched in disbelief as the tent walls vanished into the thickening grey.

She found herself standing on a vast beach, the grains of sand beneath her feet real enough to feel between her toes.

The ocean before her was a tumultuous expanse of dark blue, stretching to the horizon where the sky should meet water, but instead...

Marjie gasped.

A wave, monstrous and unforgiving, rose from the depths, its cresting higher than the tallest mountain, casting a formidable shadow that turned day into night.

Marjie's heart hammered. She turned to run, her feet sinking into the sand with each desperate step. But the beach seemed endless, and the wave gained on her. It towered above,

208

a wall of water poised to crash down and erase everything in its path.

With a roar that drowned out all thought, the tsunami descended upon her, the force of the ocean overwhelming.

Water enveloped Marjie, dragging her down into the abyssal depths. She fought against the pull, her arms flailing, reaching for a surface that was no longer there.

The pressure built around her, crushing her.

Her lungs screamed for air, but there was only water – a saline, suffocating flood that sought to claim her.

Panic clawed at her mind, each attempt to swim upwards only dragging her deeper into the watery void.

The light from above was a dim glow, growing fainter as the depths claimed her, pulling her into the cold, dark belly of the ocean...

38
AGATHA

The mist swirled around Agatha, thickening into an opaque fog that obscured her vision of the tent.

"Ridiculous!" she said and blasted it away with a spurt of air.

The fog cleared, but she found herself standing in the midst of her cherished library, the familiar scent of aged paper and leather bindings heavy in the air.

But this was not her calm sanctuary. The library had turned hostile again, the shelves trembling as a sudden wind whipped through the room, its howl a dissonant sound that set her nerves on edge. Agatha's eyes widened as books began to shudder, then, as if compelled by an unseen force, flew off the shelves in a violent frenzy.

The shelves themselves began to creak and crack into pieces.

She raised her arms to shield her face as the splinters of wood and tomes became projectiles, pages flapping wildly in the storm that raged around her.

The air was thick with words and chaos.

Struggling against the onslaught, Agatha moved with determination, pushing through the storm. Each step was met with resistance, as if the air itself sought to hold her back. She felt the sharp corners of books strike her.

Agatha knew this was no ordinary phenomenon – it was a battle of wills, her own resolve against the fears and doubts that plagued her.

With a defiant cry, Agatha pressed forward, her hands reaching out to catch a particularly large volume that hurtled towards her. She clutched it to her chest, its title embossed on the cover now clear: "Be present."

It was a sign.

39
GWYNETH

Gwyneth paced the Clochar's stone pathways, her cloak fluttering in the restless breeze. The ground beneath her feet vibrated with an erratic energy, a subtle yet unmistakable tremor that fuelled her unease. The air crackled with tension like the static before a storm.

Around her, the Clochar's usual harmony was unravelling. Voices rose in heated debate across the herb gardens, normally a place of quiet contemplation.

In the orchard, two young sisters argued vehemently, their words sharp as thorns, while others gathered in small, worried clusters.

Gwyneth approached the courtyard, her expression a mask of calm. "Sisters, let us not be swayed by fear," she implored, her voice steady. "We all sense the disturbance, but we must remain united in these troubling times."

Her words were swept away in the tide of unrest.

"We need answers, Sister Gwyneth!" a young woman retorted, her eyes blazing with defiance. "The ground itself warns us, and yet we are kept in the dark."

Something must be done...

In the fading light, the elder sisters convened in the temple, their faces etched with concern.

Gwyneth's heart was heavy with foreboding as the sky above the Clochar darkened, casting shadows across the white dwellings.

"It is time," said Sister Breag. "The magic of the Order of Crimson is threatening to breach our peace. It is a risk, not just to our sanctuary, but to the wider world. We must do what needs to be done."

"But we aren't ready, surely," said Gwyneth. "We do not yet have the Crones. We need their magic in order to activate the Veilstone."

Sister Franwen nodded. "True enough, but we do have one among us who is connected to the ancient magic. It won't bring peace to the whole world – not yet – but it will calm the Clochar."

Gwyneth shivered. "Are we certain this is the path we must take?"

"It is for the greater good," Sister Breag replied. "Peace requires difficult choices."

"But is it not a deception?" Gwyneth asked. "To bring peace to those by magic, who have not chosen it for themselves."

Franwen laughed. "Of course they would choose it; who would not choose peace?"

"Then why not give the choice to begin with?" Gwyneth asked.

Breag turned to Gwyneth, a gentle firmness in her eyes. "You know as well as I do that some knowledge is too heavy for unburdened shoulders. We must carry this weight for them."

Franwen nodded. "Our duty is to protect. The balance must be maintained, at all costs."

Gwyneth's gaze drifted towards the courtyard where the last rays of sunlight mingled with the rising tension. The murmurs of the sisters, the unsettling tremors, the air charged with apprehension – all converged into disconcerting chaos.

Sister Breag opened a small carved wooden box, revealing three amulets, silver catching in the lamp light. "Take one of these," she instructed. "They will keep our minds clear so that we can do what must be done."

Gwyneth picked up an amulet; it felt oddly light in her hands. On closer inspection it bore an emblem of the moon phases, woven with symbols of nature. She and the other elder sisters donned the amulets, and some of the unease subsided.

"I'll be back in a moment," Breag said.

Her footsteps echoed away.

"Could we not just produce more amulets?" Gwyneth asked. "For all the sisters to wear if they so choose?"

Franwen shook her head. "It will not be enough. The Order of Crimson's dark power is stirring, as you know. It is a threat to our very existence and you know what they say about desperate times..."

Breag returned but she was no longer alone. A woman walked beside her in a trance-like state, her eyes vacant yet peaceful, her white plaits drooping over her simple robes.

"Sister Matilda?" said Gwyneth, but the woman did not respond. "What happened to her?"

"She's under a spell of protection and guidance," Breag said, a note of defensiveness in her voice.

Gwyneth shook her head. "Not so long ago we were sending her on a mission out into the world to seek out the Crones..."

"And she performed that mission satisfactorily," said Franwen. "She delivered the charms. It won't be long until the Crones seek our aid and then we shall have them. Now that Mathilda has served that purpose, she has the honour of a far greater role."

Gwyneth's breath caught in her throat, but she knew better than to argue further.

"Now, we must leave," said Breag, leading them towards the entryway to the sacred tunnels beneath the temple.

Gwyneth took a deep breath. As her eyes adjusted to the darkness, the amulets they wore began emitting a soft glow, revealing more of the ancient network of passageways known only to the elder sisters.

Down here, the air was cool and damp, the walls lined with softly glowing moss that illuminated their way enough to see a few steps ahead.

The path sloped downwards at first, and then gently upward.

Sister Breag led the way, her figure a shadow against the faint luminescence that seeped from the moss clinging to the cave walls. The air carried the scent of earth and ancient stone.

In the dimness of the sacred tunnels, the world above seemed like a distant memory. The rough walls were hewn from the heart of the mountain.

The tunnels wound deep and secretive beneath the Clochar, a labyrinthine network carved by hand, both claustro-phobic and expansive at different points, the ceiling dropping low in places where they had to stoop, then opening into vast, echoing caverns.

Gwyneth followed behind Franwen, her mind adrift in the past, yet keenly aware of the present as walking through a dream.

These tunnels had witnessed the passage of countless sisters before them. Gwyneth sighed in gentle reverence in connection to those who had walked this path before her, their presence lingering in the very air she breathed.

The silence of the tunnel was deep, broken only by the soft tread of their footsteps and the distant drip of water. The sound seemed to come from everywhere and nowhere.

On and on they trod as the tunnel became more winding and narrow.

As they ascended, the air grew thinner, the passage steeper. The moss faded, and Sister Breag lit a small lantern.

The flickering flames cast a warm, golden light, creating a

dance of shadows that played across the ancient stones, revealing markings and symbols engraved into the rock.

Climbing the ancient steps, in a seemingly endless, a spiralling ascent, tested their strength, but as Sister Breag pushed open the heavy door, Gwyneth breathed a sigh of relief. Emerging from the tunnel, they were greeted by starlight and the awe-inspiring sight of the sacred crystal structure.

The Sacred Veilstone.

It towered before them, in sacred resplendent beauty. The crystalline ring, vast and intricate, pulsed with an inner light. Its core radiated a soft, ethereal glow that bathed the mountainside.

Gwyneth approached the base of the crystal, craning her neck to take in its entirety, her hand hesitantly reaching out to touch its surface. The moment her skin made contact, a warmth spread through her fingertips, as if the crystal itself was alive with a heartbeat. Long had it been the anchor for the magic of the Veiled Sisterhood, protecting the Clochar from the conflict of the world, yet now, a stronger magic was needed, a sacrifice was required to restore the balance that had been disturbed by dark forces. Gwyneth could feel a gentle vibration, a resonance that seemed to echo the rhythm of the earth itself.

Looking up, Gwyneth could see the intricate patterns that adorned the higher facets of the Veilstone crystal, like the constellations in a night sky. It was truly a great marvel; composed of countless tiny crystal facets, each one perfectly cut and angled to catch the faintest sliver of light, forming patterns that were both geometric and organic, resembling the complex symmetry of a snowflake.

The crystal seemed to hold within it the very essence of the divine feminine.

As Gwyneth gazed up, memories of her youth came flooding back. She recalled the day she and Ingrid had first glimpsed this divine monument, their youthful curiosity leading them to a place they were forbidden to explore. Ingrid's reaction had shocked Gwyneth; shock and betrayal had torn Ingrid from the sisterhood. Gwyneth had been unable the comprehend it. The Veilstone was mysterious, yes, but it was beautiful and clearly a vessel for the divine. Ingrid had not been able to see it then; perhaps she had not wanted to. She'd been restless, always. Gwyneth had often wondered if Ingrid was already looking for an excuse to leave her, to abandon the Sisterhood, and discovering this sacred relic was the shock she needed to take flight, whereas in Gwyneth the Veilstone only ever inspired deep awe and reverence from that very first moment.

The crystal stood as a silent witness to that fateful day, the history that had diverged all those years ago, leaving Gwyneth to follow the path of the sisterhood, while Ingrid sought a different destiny.

They had been young, and reckless, but had Ingrid merely seen deeper into the mystery than Gwyneth dared to? Had Ingrid been right?

Gwyneth risked a glance towards Mathilda, still in a

peaceful trance, as Breag and Franwen argued about their next steps.

Mathilda's face now was so remarkably different to how her sister's had contorted upon seeing the crystal for the first time. Ingrid's demeanour had shifted dramatically. The colour drained from her face, her usual mischievous spark replaced by a stony, serious expression.

"Come, Gwyneth," said Sister Breag. "It is time."

Gwyneth turned to see that Mathilda was no longer standing. She had been guided into the base of the chamber, her eyes now closed, her breathing steady. Gwyneth's heart clenched as something inside her sought to rescue the poor woman from her oblivious sacrifice. Her mind raced with ways to interrupt the trudge of fate, but to question Breag now was too great a risk. Instead, Gwyneth consoled herself that Mathilda would live, even if she barely experienced it, and that her continued service would be a welcome step towards peace.

The three elder sisters encircled her, their faces solemn.

"Sister Breag," whispered Gwyneth, her voice barely audible, "Mathilda has always longed to be one of us, an elder. Yet..."

Breag nodded, her expression unchanging. "Yes, her familial ties with the traitor Ingrid bars her path. But her power is undeniable, and we need it now."

"It's a shame. She could have been a great elder, if not for her past," Franwen added regretfully.

Gwyneth felt a twinge of guilt, thinking of her own closeness to Ingrid, a bond that had once felt stronger than sisterhood. She wondered what her fellow elders would say if they knew the depth of that connection. But she pushed the thought away; those days were long gone.

Gwyneth shot one last look towards Mathilda's resting form. "Perhaps after all this is over, Mathilda's sacrifice will be enough of a test of her loyalty, and she can become an elder as she longs to be."

"Perhaps," said Breag dismissively.

They began the sacred rite, chanting in unison, their voices melding into a single, harmonious melody that filled the space, vibrating against the walls. Mathilda remained still, a conduit for the power they were about to unleash.

As their chant reached its crescendo, the crystal began to glow, its light intensifying until it filled the chamber with a blinding radiance. The energy radiated outwards, pulsating with the power of the Goddess.

"It's working!" Franwen gasped, staring up at the glowing façade of the Veilstone.

Images appeared in the crystalline surface. They watched as the magic unfolded, flowing down the mountainside to where the Clochar lay.

Franwen was right. It was working.

Gwyneth watched as glimpse after glimpse was revealed in the crystal above. The disturbing magic faded away. The unrest in the courtyard melted like butter on hot toast. The sisters who had been quarrelling and anxious, now touched by the crystal's power, found their fears dissolving, their expressions of anguish, rage, and fear vanished into a serene calm.

One by one, they dispersed, returning to their quarters in a state of peaceful contemplation.

"Behold the great power of the Goddess," Breag said, her voice filled with reverence.

"It is magnificent," Gwyneth said, truthfully. Though in her mind, far more complexities were at play.

"This is just the beginning," said Franwen, her eyes still fixed on the crystal. "The Veilstone's power, combined with the Crone magic, will bring peace to the entire world."

"They just have to take the bait first," Breag said with a twinkle in her eye.

Gwyneth watched, her heart heavy with awe and unease. The magic they had wielded was extraordinary, but the cost of such power lingered in her mind. "Yes, the peace of the Goddess is upon us," she agreed softly. Yet, deep within her, a small voice questioned: *at what cost?*

40

DELIA

Delia's feet pounded against the scorched earth, the heat from the flames licking at her heels as she ran. Her mind whirled with panic as smothering memories crashed in, each more suffocating than the last. The glorious elder grove was now a distant memory as the world around her echoed with the crackling laughter of fire.

As she fled through the fire a warm, glowing sensation began to emanate from her pocket. She reached inside, fingers brushing lightly against paper and petals – the envelope charm from Merryn and Keyne. The warmth of their love for her radiated outwards and a realisation dawned in Delia's mind, piercing the haze of her fear. The flames did not consume nor did the smoke choke. The trees stood tall and unharmed, untouched by the blaze. It was a mirage. Delia stopped running, her breaths ragged, as she forced herself to face the inferno.

She closed her eyes, focusing on the beat of her heart, the rhythm grounding her to reality. As she reopened them, the flames seemed to hesitate, their menacing presence faltering under her newfound scrutiny. With each steady breath, Delia asserted control, and the fire retreated, its ferocity waning until it dissipated into nothingness, revealing a new truth – she was no longer anywhere near the elder grove, no longer surrounded by trees at all.

Snowflakes fell softly around her. The ground was blanketed in white, and the air was sharp with the bite of cold. Delia wrapped her arms around herself, grateful she'd never thought to remove her winter coat.

Disoriented and with no sense of direction, she began to walk. The snow muffled her steps, the world around her a silent expanse of white.

Wind shipped around her as the snowstorm picked up.

Time became a blur as she trudged on, her thoughts as scattered as the snowflakes that swirled around her. She needed to find the others...or find somewhere safe and potentially warm to shelter until the storm passed. Just as her hope waned, a dark shape emerged in the distance, visible through the blizzard – a hut – a beacon in the desolate landscape.

With renewed energy, Delia pressed on towards the promise of shelter.

41
DECLAN

A vast expanse of white stretched out before Declan. His breath hung lightly in the air like a cloud while the orders from the Shepherd weighed heavily on him. They chafed against his sense of duty. They asked of him actions that went beyond the scope of his contract; he was a rogue tracker, not a pawn in their game of control.

His magic, a subtle thrumming at the back of his mind, had alerted him as soon as Delia had left Myrtlewood. At that moment, it wasn't the Order that had filled his thoughts, but a gnawing concern for the solitary figure now venturing into the heart of the storm.

He knew where she was, in theory. He'd been following his magic towards this very place, yet he hadn't anticipated the sense of relief – the weight leaving his shoulders as they slumped forward at the sight of her.

Alone, she was a figure of resilience against the vastness white landscape, moving with purpose towards a distant hut.

No one should be alone out here, even Delia, with her fierce spirit and the troubles that seemed to gravitate towards her.

He was certain she had no desire to see him, that his presence was as welcome as the biting cold. She'd thrown him out of that public house with a fiery rage rivalling any force he'd encountered in his long life.

Yet, he couldn't ignore the pull of his own conscience, the need to understand why she was here, exposed to the elements and to dangers untold.

Declan adjusted his cloak, squinting against the flurry that had begun to obscure his vision. She was getting closer to the hut, a safe haven against the storm, but the snow was falling faster now, the wind howling like a chorus of wraiths. In a storm such as this, even solid buildings could vanish from view – the flurries could distract and mislead the senses. If he didn't act soon, she might disappear into the white, lost to him and to the world.

With a silent apology for the intrusion he was about to make, Declan trod onwards, picking up his pace, closing the distance between them.

He had to reach her, whether it was wanted or not.

It wasn't just about the Order, anymore, or his own struggle with his ancient pact. It was something more, though he could not name it, not exactly.

The storm cleared and Delia's figure became more visible in the distance, resolute against the snow. She was not yet aware of his approach, her focus fixed on her destination. Declan prepared himself, ready to face a challenge more daunting than the storm that raged around them.

42

DELIA

Delia's footsteps crunched in the snow as she approached the cabin. Her breath formed little puffs of mist in the cold air, and she shivered, pulling her coat tighter around her. She pushed open the creaky door and stepped into the dim interior, taking a moment to absorb the details of the rustic space. It seemed seldom used, perhaps abandoned, but now it was a refuge from the storm and it might as well have been the Ritz for the comfort and relief it offered her in that moment.

A gust of wind howled through the gaps in the wooden walls. Shadows shifted on walls, cast by the faint light that struggled to shine through the dusty, frosted windows.

Her eyes settled on the unlit fireplace.

Perfect.

Footsteps sounded outside and Delia froze.

Fearing the worst, she retreated to a shadowy corner of the room, her heart pounding with thoughts of the Order.

The door swung open, and a man stepped in.

She recognised him immediately from the silhouette of his hat.

The cowboy.

Declan stepped in, shaking snow from his boots.

"Get out!" Delia's voice was sharp.

"I was...just checking on you," Declan replied, his brows furrowed. "What in the name of all gods are you doing out here alone with a storm brewing?"

"Why do you care?" Delia shot back, crossing her arms defensively.

Declan's face twisted with anger. "You've bewitched me, Delia."

Declan's posture was rigid, his eyes were narrow slits of suspicion, and Delia's face flushed, not from warmth but from rising rage.

"Bewitched you?" She laughed bitterly. "I can barely control my powers, let alone use them to bewitch someone."

He took a step closer, his voice low and intense. "I can't stop thinking about you. You've stirred something in me I can't control."

Delia, taken aback, said, "How dare you make that my problem. If you can't control your rage, you need anger management. It's nothing to do with me!"

A heavy silence filled the room with its weight.

"It's everything to do with you," he insisted, moving towards the fireplace.

"What are you doing?" she asked, eyeing him warily.

"Lighting the fire. We'll freeze otherwise." Declan's hands fumbled with the damp kindling, the musty smell of wet wood filling the cabin. "The wood's damp. This might take a while."

Delia glanced sharply at the fireplace, and the damp wood ignited instantly.

There was a moment of silence as the flames took hold, casting a warm glow over the room.

Declan glanced over his shoulder, impressed. "I should have thought of that," he admitted.

"It seems you should have thought of more than that," Delia replied, her arms still crossed.

"What were you were thinking?" Declan asked, rage building in his voice. "Wandering alone in a snowstorm...Have you no respect for your mortality?"

Delia, feeling a spark of boldness, unfolded her arms and stepped closer to Declan, her gaze locked with his. "And what about you?" she challenged. "Have you thought about why you're really here? Or are you just going to stand there blaming me or the Order or something else rather than taking responsibility for your actions?"

Declan took a step back, as if scorched by her words. "You have no idea what you're talking about," he muttered.

"I should burn you to cinders right now," Delia spat out.

"It wouldn't help," Declan responded calmly.

"It would help a great deal right now." She glared at him.

"Why haven't you done it then? You've had the chance," he asked, challenging her.

The crackling of the fire punctuated the stillness, its sporadic pops and hisses. Outside, the wind had died down, leaving a hush over the cabin.

"Why indeed..." Delia's frustration morphed into a different kind of energy. She approached the fireplace, her movements deliberate, and picked up the cast iron poker. Turning it over in her hands, she looked back at Declan. "I'm not sure I can bear this."

"I'll make sure you survive the storm, whatever it takes," he said earnestly.

Delia paused, her anger wavering for a moment. "It's not the storm I'm worried about."

She turned towards him, her eyes taking him in as if seeking to quench a long-held thirst, a hunger.

In that instant, Declan stepped forward.

The air between them seemed to crackle like the fire in the hearth. Delia's heart raced, her breath caught in her throat.

Delia shook herself. She was too old and wise to swoon, surely. She needed to find her friends, and she needed to get back safely to Myrtlewood, and she had to survive this snow-storm...She had a million things on her mind, but they all vanished as her hunger took over.

She reached for him.

Simultaneously, Declan reached out, his hands gently but firmly grasping her arms. With a surprising gentleness, he pushed her against the rough wooden wall of the cabin.

Delia's back pressed against the cold, uneven surface, the sensation contrasting sharply with the warmth of Declan's body so close to hers. She looked up at him, her eyes wide with surprise, fear, and an undeniable flicker of something else...

"What is it with you pushing me against walls?" she asked. "You did the same thing when you tried to stop me entering that theatre in London."

"What is it with you and dangerous situations?"

Delia shrugged. "You know what they say...fight fire with fire?"

"That's the worst advice I've ever heard. Declan's gaze was intense, burning into hers, as if searching for an answer or perhaps permission in her eyes.

"This is...different," Delia said, her words wholly insufficient to describe the fluttering in her chest or the way the world seemed to warp around them in that moment.

"You're not going to burn me like you did in London, are you?" he asked with a tone of warm humour.

Delia laughed. "We'll see."

For a heartbeat, they were frozen, the air thick with tension and unspoken words. Declan's gaze bore into hers, searching, questioning, demanding an answer she wasn't sure she had.

The world seemed to pause, the crackling of the fire the only sound in the room. Then, slowly, almost hesitantly, Declan leaned in.

A part of Delia still wanted to resist, to set him on fire and run away, but she hesitated as another part of her psyche called to her. It wanted nothing more than to dive into this man who smelled of woodsmoke and wild herbs. Her mind protested, filled with all the things she ought to be concerned about, but her deeper cravings overcame her – to devour like a raging fire fed dry kindling and to be devoured in turn.

She let go her doubt and let her thirst take the reins, pulling Declan towards her like a cool drink of water in a dry desert.

When their lips finally met, it was with a passion that was as fierce as it was unexpected, a furnace of sensations, tumultuous and fiery, powered by the same rage and frustration that had fuelled their words, yet there was an undercurrent of something more, a depth of feeling that Delia hadn't allowed herself to acknowledge until now.

This man was working for the Order – her sworn enemies and her horrendous ex-husband – yet all along he'd subtly thwarted them, or was that her imagination? Was the attraction she'd been suppressing for Declan just another manipulation? Was the Order still messing with her mind, puppeteering her life?

Delia's mind reeled, caught between the urge to push him away and the desire to pull him closer.

No...this wasn't Jerry's doing. This wasn't the Order at work. She was sure of it. This was something more natural, primal, instinctual.

Her hands, which had initially balled into fists at her sides, slowly uncurled, tentatively resting against Declan's chest. His heart pounded a rapid drumbeat that matched her own.

She now gripped the fabric of his shirt, torn between resistance and the unexpected urge to pull him closer as her thoughts scattered to the winds of the building storm.

43
DECLAN

Declan's world narrowed to the feel of Delia Spark's lips against his. It was an impulsive move, a reckless act that sent shockwaves through his senses.

He drew back, aghast at his own behavior. This woman was dangerous...and yet...

Delia's response was fierce, her kiss a blaze that threatened to burn through the bond that held him to his magic.

Declan stumbled backwards, his mind racing. "I can't," he gasped, the words catching in his throat. "Breaking my oath... it's too dangerous. I could lose my powers."

Delia glared at him, her passion quickly turning back to rage. "Your powers?"

"Breaking the oath with my work – my contract – risks losing my magic." He stumbled over the words, trying to make them make sense in a situation that was progressively growing more insane.

Delia's glare intensified. "Do you know what kind of problems your powers have caused? You've tracked me all over the place to aid that horrific Order of Crimson. To hell with your powers!"

Declan saw the tremble in her lips, betraying more complex emotions.

"You don't understand," he said. "And maybe you don't care to."

Delia slumped against the wall. "Try me."

"My powers saved me...long ago. They're the only thing that keeps me from madness."

"And you think this"—she gestured between them—"whatever this is with us...you think it will destroy them."

Declan let out a long slow sigh, the tension leaving his shoulders a little. It had been a long time since he'd shared his inner burdens with anyone. He didn't know how much he could tell Delia, but something nudged him forward into sharing more. "A long time ago I was cursed, and then blessed. The blessings of my powers help to make the curse bearable, but they are tied to my work. You have no idea how much I've wanted to break the contract on you – the contract with the Order. It has driven me to the edges of madness, and yet..."

"You're saying taking things any further with me will drive you insane?" Delia folded her arms defensively.

"I'm saying that these two things cannot co-exist. I cannot

unite with you and also work against you. Love will break the bond of the contract."

Delia scoffed. "Who said anything about love?"

Declan cast his gaze down towards the floor. Perhaps this was nothing to her – this vibrant, worldly woman who had so much to live for. Perhaps it was just lust, and yet he knew in his bones that this was a connection unlike others he had encountered. Despite his long life, he could not fathom the mysteries of love, but he knew it instinctually. He could not deny it. He had been working against the Order, subtly undermining them from the very beginning, because this woman stirred something deeper within him. Perhaps his magic had already begun dissipating. His mind certainly couldn't think straight.

She stepped closer, reducing the distance between them to a mere whisper.

"What if it's worth the risk?" Delia asked, her gaze softening, yet her eyes pierced into his soul.

"How could it be?" he asked bitterly.

"You're not happy, going around in circles. The Order will never let you go – you're too valuable to them. They have you bound, and they know it."

Declan shrugged. "Things change. People die."

He couldn't tell her of his immortality, he'd vowed to himself never to reveal that truth again, not to anyone, not after the last time. When people knew of his curse they told others, word spread, and some people always took it upon themselves to do their best to test it. He'd undergone more agonising torture over the centuries than he cared to reflect upon.

Delia shook her head. "The Order won't die, they'll come back like a never-ending encore."

He didn't want to tell her the thought in his mind. *Perhaps not, but you will...* The contract was on Delia Spark, after all. And the Shepherd meant to end it now, one way or another. His eyes had been cold through the seer's stone as he'd demanded her capture – dead or alive.

Yet, Declan could not bring himself to think of her death. If that was the only way the contract could end, he didn't want it.

He felt the heat of her body, the intensity in her gaze. "Could it be worth testing, Declan?" she asked. "I take it you've never broken a contract before."

He shook his head, slowly. "But that was the condition of my blessing – my powers are bound to my work."

"What do you have to lose other than this madness?" she asked.

In that moment, as he gazed into Delia's eyes, filled with yearning and uncertainty, Declan's resolve wavered.

Declan, caught in a storm of uncertainty and longing, pondered the weight of her words. Despite her lack of understanding of the full gravity of their situation, he found himself questioning whether the risk might, indeed, be justifiable. Yielding to the magnetic pull between them.

The risk, the fear, the oath – everything paled in the intensity of their connection.

He leaned in, his senses alight with the spicy scent of her, the warmth of her skin.

"Maybe it is," he murmured before their lips met again in a fiery, passionate kiss.

They moved closer to the rug by the fire, consumed by an inferno of desire.

The fire crackled in the hearth, casting patterns of shadows and light across Delia's face, illuminating her features in a haunting, ethereal glow. The orange light flickered in her eyes, revealing depths of emotion he had never seen before. The air was thick with the scent of burning wood, mingling with the faint trace of Delia's perfume.

The memory of the day he took his oath flashed in his mind, a vivid reminder of what was at stake.

Declan lost himself in the moment, surrendering to the crucible of passion and rage and irrevocable change as the bond within him, the oath he'd taken to his work, the very fibre of his magic, began to unravel.

The world seemed to fracture around them. Declan was plunging into darkness, the pact that bound him breaking under the power of connection.

As his magic disintegrated, Declan felt the dust and decay of centuries begin to peel away from his soul, clearing the burdens of his existence, each particle a memory, a moment of time now liberated; the remnants of a life lived in the shadows of duty and servitude, lifted from him, the exodus leaving a void where once there had been boundless power.

In this experience of annihilation, as Declan teetered on the brink of nonexistence, a warmth began to infiltrate the cold emptiness. A light, faint yet resolute, pierced through the encompassing darkness.

Delia.

Her essence, her fiery spirit, reached out across the void, a lifeline cast into the depths of his despair. The thought of her, the memory of her presence, ignited a spark within the vast darkness...Connection.

Yet who was he now to deserve such bounty? He was nothing.

Terror surged within him. He had sacrificed his very magic in a moment of passion, leaving him with the knowledge that he was now nothing but one thing he most despised: his enduring immortality.

44

DELIA

T he tension that had been simmering between them for weeks erupted as she and Declan collided. Delia found herself engulfed in sensation – she still had resistance – the fear and anger, but now it was joined by unexpected, overwhelming desire.

When Declan's lips found hers, a spark ignited, setting her alight from within.

She trembled, not from fear, but from the intensity more potent than any spell she'd known. In that instant, all the conflict, the fiery arguments and clashes, dissolved into an all-consuming need.

Delia realised how much she craved this closeness, this raw, physical connection that she'd denied herself for so long. Every touch, every kiss, reignited something inside her she thought had been lost to the follies of youth.

Declan's hands guided her gently to the rug by the fire, their bodies silhouetted against the flickering flames. Each kiss was a spark that fuelled her growing passion, a fire that threatened to consume them both.

As he revealed himself to her, layer by layer, through the depths of emotion in his eyes and the language of his body, Delia surrendered to a transformation within herself.

Her hostility towards him had been a shield, protecting her – not from the Order, as she'd mistakenly believed – but from something far more terrifying: her own vulnerability.

The resentment and defences she had built up over time now melted away, leaving her exposed and open.

The sensations washed over her, intense pleasure and pain, a tidal wave of bliss that built to an unbearable intensity.

Outside, the wind howled, as if nature itself was responding to the intensity of their union. The old hut creaked and groaned under the strain.

She felt the surge of Declan's magic, a shift in the air, a tingling that coursed through her body. Looking into his eyes, she glimpsed a vast, ancient void, a mystery too deep to fathom.

Carried away by the wave of sensations, Delia lost herself in a moment of pure, unbridled joy. As Declan's voice echoed in the room, she felt a final, shattering shift, a burst of magic.

It was only then that his words came back to her along with the burden of his sacrifice.

She looked into his eyes and sensed a terrifying darkness.

She had lost herself, momentarily, but had he lost his magic for good?

45
MARJIE

"Thank goodness those blasted illusions passed quickly," Marjie said, searching her heart for shreds of cheer to tie together to make the situation bearable.

Inside the tent where the crones sat, the air was infused with the calming scent of tea and the rich, oaky aroma of sherry, the former comforts now mingling with an air of embattled reflection. The three women sat, their cups cradled in their hands as they processed the terrifying and haunting visions that had so recently tormented them.

Marjie she reached out to pat the dragon puppy for comfort, while her mind circled back to Delia. Where on earth was she? Had she run away from them or been chased by the very same illusions that had plagued each of the other crones, drawing on their deepest fears.

"That was a rather strange turn of events," said Ingrid. "To put it mildly."

Marjie let out a long sigh, the steam from her tea curling up into the air. "Yes, after that adventure, I might need something a bit stronger than tea," she remarked, eyeing the Agatha's bottle of sherry with a new level of appreciation.

Agatha, leaned back against a cushion with a smirk. "Marjie speaking sense? I'll need to mark the calendar. And I thought I'd only live to see flying books."

Marjie shot Agatha a playful glare, hoping the banter would sooth her nerves after the terrifying mirage, and ease her worries about Delia.

Ingrid shook her head. "If we survive this quest, it will be no thanks to your bickering."

Marjie wrapped her hands tighter around her teacup. "I never thought I'd live to see the day where I'd dive deeply into the ocean, I usually can't even stand to get near enough to dip my toes in."

Ingrid nodded sagely. "And I faced down a dragon larger than this tent. It's funny, isn't it? Our fears, when given form, are more formidable than any beast of legend."

Agatha let out a dry laugh. "My illusion was only a slightly more intense version of the mess my library keeps turning into in reality at the whim of my wayward powers. What does that say about me?"

Marjie chuckled. "Trust you to be too stubborn to have an illusion outside of your daily reality."

Agatha glared. "At least my books have substance, Marjie.

They're not filled with make-believe and...whatever it is you fill your pot with."

Ingrid raised an eyebrow, interjecting with a smirk, "Marjie fills her pot with hope and a good dash of recklessness, it seems. Just what we need to keep us on our toes."

The conversation ebbed and flowed but danced around the absence that they all clearly felt. Marjie, in her heightened empathy, could tell the others were just as rattled as she was, not only by the illusions but also by Delia's continued absence.

"You know," Marjie said, setting down her cup with a decisive clink, "I always thought drowning in a sea of emotion was just a figure of speech."

Ingrid laughed, a sound as grounding as the earth itself. "And I always believed I had a firm footing in this world. But that cliff...well, it had other ideas."

Marjie glanced back to the empty chair. "I can't help but worry about Delia. Out there all alone, with no idea where she is..."

Ingrid reached across, placing a reassuring hand on Marjie's. "Scry for her, Marjie. You have the power and the heart. Let it guide you."

Reluctance flickered through Marjie's mind. She wasn't sure about using her magic now, not with everything that had happened, but Ingrid insisted.

With a resigned nod, Marjie accepted the bowl of water Ingrid provided, setting it before her with a steadying breath. She lit a candle, its flickering flame casting a glow that steadied her resolve.

She whispered an invocation, her words a gentle caress over the surface of the water.

The image materialised swiftly. "I see a fireplace," Marjie announced, relief washing over her. "Delia is safe. She's found shelter and...oh!" A sudden blush bloomed on her cheeks, and with a sweep of her hand, the image was gone.

"What is it?" Agatha leaned in, her curiosity piqued by Marjie's sudden coyness.

"Never you mind," Marjie said. "Delia is...well. We can stay here for the night and look for her in the morning."

Ingrid's eyes twinkled with amusement. "Some secrets are best kept even from friends, eh, Marjie?"

Marjie, recovering her composure, shot back, "My dear, some secrets are like Agatha's cooking. Best avoided at all costs!"

46

DECLAN

Morning light filtered through the grimy windows of the hut, shining across the worn wooden floor. Declan rummaged through his bag, his movements methodical, the familiarity of the routine grounding him after the unsettling events of the previous night. He prepared a simple meal using ingredients he'd been gifted by a grateful farmer he'd helped out during his recent travels – sourdough bread, a bit of cheese, and tea – the scent of the brew a subtle comfort in the silence of the hut.

Delia sat across from him, her expression thoughtful, wrapped in the warmth of the tea cupped between her hands.

"I don't know what to make of last night," she admitted, breaking the stillness that hung between them.

Declan remained silent, his response a mere nod. His mind

was a blur of thoughts – uncertainly and the weight of his broken contract with the Order bearing down on him.

"You seem distant," Delia said with a hit of challenge in her voice. "Like a wall has come down. I'm not saying last night means anything in particular, but I don't go in for the silent, broody, aloof types."

Declan allowed himself a small, sly smile. "Are you meaning to deceive me with that comment, or yourself?"

Delia's response was a playful shove, her smile a brief flicker of ease in the tension that filled the room.

She took a sip of her tea, the warmth of the liquid a small comfort. "Thank you for this," she said softly.

He nodded again, his gaze lingering on her for a moment before looking away.

The silence stretched between them, each lost in their reflections.

"Your powers..." Delia began, breaking the quiet. Her voice was hesitant, probing.

Declan cast his eyes down, the admission heavy on his tongue. "I felt the contract snap. It's broken...all of it."

"But how do you know?" Delia asked.

He shook his head, resignation and relief in his gesture. "I just do."

Delia rolled her eyes. "You're not even going to test them?"

Accepting the challenge, Declan reached for his knuckle-bones, the tools of his trade. "Who should I locate?"

"The other crones," Delia replied. "I got lost last night. There was some kind of illusion, and I found myself in the middle of nowhere." She narrowed her eyes at him. "It was probably the Order up to no good again. You wouldn't know anything about that, would you?"

"I'm afraid not," Declan replied. "They didn't tend to inform me of their plans unless I needed to know some particular detail."

Delia sighed, a reluctant trust in her eyes. "The strange thing is, I believe you, despite all the reasons not to. Go on, test those powers. Find the crones. Don't tell the Order where they are."

"I no longer work for the Order," Declan said, feeling the last of the tension drain from his shoulders. "Powers or not, at least I'm free."

Delia nudged him, pulling his attention back towards the objects in his hand.

He focused on the knucklebones, concentrating.

Nothing...

He sighed.

All was lost.

Delia reached out to comfort him and he surrendered to her gentle touch. In that moment, he relaxed and a familiar sensation coursed through him, tingling down his arm to his palm where the bones still rested.

The magic worked.

A smile spread across Delia's face as she watched tiny sparkles dancing around the bones, but she remained silent.

Declan closed his eyes as the images came to him. "I've found them. It's not far, an hour's walk or so."

He opened his eyes to see Delia grinning at him. "You have your powers!"

"So it seems," Declan replied, his eyes meeting hers. "And now I'm free..."

"That's wonderful!"

He smiled at her. "You...are wonderful."

Delia blushed and looked down at her cup. "I supposed I'd better get walking."

"I can portal you there," Declan offered, a slight hesitation in his voice. "If it works...It will give me a chance to test my magic again, and perhaps you'd like to linger a while before you leave."

Delia's blush deepened.

47

INGRID

Ingrid stepped out of the tent, her eyes widening once more with wonder at the beauty of the majestic elder grove. The vibrant greens and golds were mesmerising as the sunlight. The air was alive with the scent of earth and wild herbs. The sacred grove filled her with peace after the rather tumultuous evening they'd had.

Agatha followed Ingrid out of the tent, scanning the area, her eyes lighting up again in the face of the grove's exquisite beauty. "Any sign of clues as to what we're looking for?" she asked. "Surely there's something hidden in this magical place that will help find the air dragon."

"Why the air dragon?" Marjie asked. "The signs could be leading us anywhere..."

"Because this place was hinted at in my grimoire and I'm the air crone," Agatha insisted, crossing her arms stubbornly.

Marjie merely shrugged. "All I'm saying is that we have no idea of anything, really."

Agatha puffed out a breath. "Speak for yourself. I'm determined to find my dragon. Let's get to it."

"Perhaps we could fetch Delia first," Ingrid suggested. "She might be helpful, after all."

Marjie, who was already meandering among the trees with childlike curiosity, called back, "Oh, let's give Delia a bit more time, shall we? I do believe she needs a little space right now."

Ingrid raised an eyebrow at that, but swiftly her gaze was drawn to a cluster of stones that glinted in the sunlight. "Look here!" she exclaimed. "These stones...Could they be part of a map?"

The crones gathered around the stones. Their arrangement seemed both mysterious and intriguing to Ingrid.

She leaned closer, trying to discern a pattern. "Agatha, with your all your logic and scholarly knowledge, can't you make sense of this?"

Agatha peered at the stones, her brow furrowed in concentration. "Well, if we consider the orientation of the grove and the position of the sun..." She trailed off, lost in thought.

Marjie, lounging against a tree, interjected, "You know, sometimes you just have to feel these things. Maybe the stones are less of a map and more of a...what do you call it, a spiritual GPS?"

Ingrid laughed. "A spiritual GPS? Marjie, only you could come up with something like that."

Agatha huffed, "Intuition over logic? That's like choosing a dowsing rod over a compass. But, considering our chaotic track record, Marjie's 'spiritual GPS' might just lead us somewhere."

Ingrid stared at the stones, captivated by their arrangement.

Bathed in dapples of sunlight that broke through the leafy canopy, the pebbles sparkled, catching the light and reflecting it in tiny brilliant sparks.

The stones were an assortment of shapes and sizes, some smooth and rounded by the passage of time, others jagged and raw, as if freshly hewn from the earth.

They were laid out in a pattern that was clearly deliberate, a design that seemed to resonate with hidden meaning.

Ingrid's eyes traced the lines between the stones. Could this be a map? The way the stones were aligned, they could be interpreted as creating a series of interconnected pathways, each leading to a central point marked by a particularly large, flat stone that glowed warmly in the sunlight.

The more she looked, the more the arrangement took on the appearance of a star chart or a diagram of celestial bodies, as if the stones were a mirror of the sky above, a reflection of the constellations that had guided travellers and mystics throughout the ages.

Yet, there was more to it than just a map of the heavens. Ingrid sensed a deeper connection, a link to the very essence of the grove and the ancient magic it harboured.

Her thoughts drifted to her youth and the teachings of the Clochar, to the lore of the natural world and the mystical forces that bound it.

The grove was a living entity, a nexus of power, and the stones, she surmised, were like nodes in a vast network of energy. Perhaps, in understanding their arrangement, they could tap into the ancient wisdom of this sacred place.

Ingrid's gaze settled once more on the central stone. It was a symbol, a focal point that beckoned to her intuition, to the part of her that understood the language of the earth.

As she pondered the stones, the sunlight shifted, casting new patterns of light and shadow. Ingrid watched, her heart open to the whispers of the grove, ready to receive the clues that would unravel the mystery.

Ingrid crouched down and tapped the centre stone with her finger, musing aloud. "Something about this place brings out the little child hidden within me – like I could stay here all day playing make-believe."

48

AGATHA

Agatha found herself once again transfixed by the majesty of the grove as they observed the pebbles glinting in on the ground, illuminated by the golden light filtering through the giant elder trees.

A light breeze caught her attention and she looked up at the stunning canopy above, raising her arms as if to catch some of the magic and take it with her.

Marjie playfully nudged her, eyes sparkling with mischief. "Agatha, stop your lollygagging! If it's the air dragon we're after, shouldn't you be the one to work this out? Perhaps you could tap into your intuition."

Agatha shot her a withering look. "Intuition? Marjie, I think you're mistaking me for someone else. I don't have any of that. In fact, I don't even believe in it."

Marjie leaned closer to Agatha, a playful grin on her face.

"Oh, come on. Even the logic-driven Agatha must have a tiny bit of intuition."

Ingrid chuckled. "Perhaps it's so deeply buried that it's become a legend. 'The Lost Intuition of Agatha' – sounds like a mystery waiting to be solved."

Agatha cleared her throat. "Very funny. You might as well assume I have a hidden talent for singing opera. If intuition were a book, I'd have read it cover to cover. But as it stands, it's more like a blank page."

Marjie winked at Ingrid. "I'd pay good money to see Agatha sing opera. But seriously, sometimes logic needs a little nudge from the heart, Agatha. These stones, they're more than just pieces in a puzzle; they're part of something greater, something we feel rather than deduce."

Ingrid nodded in agreement, her gaze thoughtful. "Marjie's right, Agatha. Sometimes, what we seek isn't in the realm of the tangible. This grove is ancient; it holds secrets that logic alone can't unravel."

Agatha sighed, a reluctant smile tugging at her lips. "Alright, I'll play along with this intuition game. But if I start singing opera, I'm blaming both of you."

Agatha stood closed her eyes, allowing the soft breeze to brush across her skin. Without the sight of the beautiful grove to distract her, all her usual worries and mental tensions crowded back in.

Around her, the ancient trees stood silent, as if bearing witness to her internal struggle.

She took a deep breath, focusing on the sensations around

her – the gentle rustle of leaves, the warmth of the sun filtering through the canopy, the earthy scent of the grove.

In that moment of stillness, she confronted her frustration head-on. It was true; she was intellectually bothered, agitated by the ambiguity of the stones and the uncertainty of their task. But as she delved deeper into her thoughts, she realised that it was the ambiguity – the uncertainty itself – that unsettled her.

The unknown had always been her adversary, a challenge to her logical mind.

Marjie spoke softly, her voice gently rippling through Agatha's mind. "Perhaps acceptance is the key."

Agatha had to admit there was wisdom in those words. She had spent so much of her life clinging to the concrete, the provable, yet here in the grove, surrounded by mysteries that defied explanation, she was forced to confront a different reality.

In that moment she acknowledged her limitations, the simple truth that despite her vast knowledge and logical acumen, she didn't – and couldn't – know everything, and she certainly couldn't *understand* everything.

The world was full of unknowns, mysteries that no amount of logic could unravel. And in that there was a certain freedom, a release from the need to always have the answers. In fact, there was a pleasure in the wide open space of the unfathomable, even if that pleasure came with a distinct discomfort to her sense of importance.

With her eyes still closed, Agatha felt a shift within her, a subtle loosening of the bonds that her need for certainty had placed around her.

She even embraced her frustration in her lack of understanding, and her resentment of the deeper truth that, like all human beings, her perception was limited.

When she finally opened her eyes, the grove seemed different, as if her acceptance had changed not just her inner world, but the world around her. The stones now appeared to her as a beautiful enigma, not a puzzle to be solved but something to be experienced.

Ingrid and Marjie watched her, a knowing look passing between them.

Perhaps they understood that Agatha had crossed a threshold, stepping into a realm where intuition held as much value as intellect, where accepting the unknown was as important as concrete truth.

As Agatha stood in quiet acceptance, something extraordinary began to unfold around them. One by one, each stone started to glimmer more brightly, as if awakening from a long slumber.

The glimmering grew into a steady, pulsating glow, the stones emitting a warm, golden light that seemed to breathe and expand with a life of its own.

"Agatha, you've done it!" Marjie exclaimed.

"What have I done?" Agatha asked, her eyes wide as she turned to witness the spectacle unfolding before them.

"Whatever the secret code was," Marjie said, her gaze fixed on the glowing stones. "You've unlocked it!"

The golden light intensified, becoming brighter and more radiant with each passing moment, swirling around the stones, forming a vortex of sparkling luminescence.

"It's not a map after all," Ingrid said with awe. "It's a portal."

The light twisted and twined, weaving an archway that stood tall amidst the grove, a gateway of pure, golden brilliance.

The air around the portal seemed to hum with energy, a force that resonated with the ancient power of the grove. The light from it cast ethereal shadows, painting the earth and trees in hues of amber and violet as if the grove was awakening.

As the crones watched, mesmerised, the portal's light grew more coherent, its edges becoming defined and clear.

The sparkling golden light took on a tangible quality as if woven from liquid gold, framing the vivid image which appeared within: blue sky peppered with clouds.

The air was charged with anticipation and wonder, and for a moment, time itself seemed to stand still, waiting for their next move.

Agatha stepped forward, right to the edge of the portal, staring into the expanse of sky that lay beyond it.

Her eyes narrowed in suspicion.

"What tomfoolery is this?" she muttered, her usual scepticism surfacing.

Marjie, ever the encourager, nudged her gently. "It's your leap of faith, Agatha. Go on."

Ingrid, her expression thoughtful, interjected, "What about Delia? Shouldn't we fetch her first?"

Agatha, with a shiver of fear, eagerly agreed. "Yes! Delia. We really should wait for her."

But Marjie shook her head, a sly grin on her face. "I believe Delia is...occupied. Let's just say, she's in good hands."

Ingrid, her patience waning, stepped forward. "Let's just get on with it then, and see what's there. Marjie's right. We don't know how long this portal will last."

Agatha sighed. "Would you like to try it, Ingrid?"

Ingrid shook her head. "Agatha, I do believe you must go first."

Agatha's face paled slightly. "What if it's a trick?" she stammered, her eyes darting between the portal and her companions.

Ingrid's voice was firm, reassuring. "It isn't a trick, Agatha. Of that, I'm certain."

"As I've just come to understand, nothing is ever certain, except that I'm afraid of heights," Agatha replied, her voice trembling a little.

She squared her shoulders, bracing herself she cast one last firm glance at Ingrid. "Catch me with your magic if I fall."

She took a deep breath of determination and trepidation.

Then, with a courage that surprised even herself, Agatha stepped forward and took her leap of faith, plunging into the portal and into the wide open sky.

49

DELIA

It was time for Delia to leave the hut and to leave Declan behind – to find the other crones. Delia knew this, but first, she had to find her clothes!

Delia rummaged through the dusty contents of the hut, searching for scattered items, wishing she knew that brilliant cleaning spell to get rid of the grime.

Each garment she found and slipped into felt like a step back into reality, after a night that had been anything but ordinary.

As she dressed, a knot formed in her chest, a tangle of embarrassment, excitement, and confusion.

Her time with Declan had been unexpected, to say the least. Their tensions, which had built to a fever pitch, had melted away in a series of moments that now played vividly in her mind.

She shook her head, chiding herself. *What was I thinking? I'm a grandmother, for crying out loud.* Yet another voice inside her argued, *but why can't grandmothers have fun too?*

Declan had been fairly quiet. Perhaps he was always like that. Delia hardly knew him, after all.

Was he a witch, or some other creature? The various unknowns sent a shiver down her spine.

Finally dressed, she turned to him. "I need to go," she said firmly.

"Right now?" he asked.

She nodded. "Thank you for..." Her voice trailed off, unsure how to define what had transpired between them.

"It was an honour to spend the night with you," Declan said.

"Err, good. Right, can you send me to the elder grove or wherever the crones are now?"

Declan's steely gaze met hers, and for a moment, the world seemed to melt away again. Delia quickly shook herself free of the spell. *I don't have time for this.*

He nodded, reaching for his small pouch of bones. "I'll check."

"Thank you," Delia said, feeling strangely small and young in that moment.

As he cast his magic, a frown creased Declan's forehead. "What is it?" Delia asked.

"They've moved, but the new location is...odd," Declan replied.

Panic fluttered in Delia's chest. While she had been losing

herself in a moment of unexpected passion, the crones were on the move. Were they in trouble?

"Can you cast a portal?" she asked urgently. "Please."

Declan wasted no time; his movements were precise as he worked his magic once more. "Let's hope this works," he muttered, then breathed a small sigh of relief as the air quivered, and a portal began to form, its edges glowing with a deep blue light.

Before stepping through, Delia turned back. "You'd better stay and not follow," she said, her tone leaving no room for argument.

He nodded, respecting her wishes. "For now," he agreed, a hint of something unreadable in his voice.

Delia took a deep breath and stepped into the portal. The golden light engulfed her, followed by miles of unending blue and white...and for a brief moment, she hung there, suspended in the sky.

50
GWYNETH

Gwyneth's footsteps echoed softly on the worn stones as she approached the moonlit temple. The cool night are caressed her skin. Around her, the grounds of the Clochar glowed with a pearlescent sheen.

As she entered the temple's main hall, she sensed the atmosphere, charged with tension, the air heavy with the scent of jasmine and myrrh.

Sisters Breag and Franwen awaited her, their figures silhouetted against the white temple walls. They stood by the altar, a simple stone structure that bore the marks of countless ceremonies.

Breag turned to Gwyneth as she approached. "Ah, Sister Gwyneth. Thank you for coming promptly. We have matters to discuss of much importance."

"So important they could not be discussed by the light of

day?" Gwyneth raised an eyebrow.

Sister Breag's lips tightened. "Indeed. It is time I filled you in on the full plan that Sister Mathilda set in motion."

"The plan to lure the Crones here?" Gwyneth said. "What more is there to know?"

Franwen's mouth curled into a smile. It seemed she had already been in on the scheme, perhaps right from the beginning. Breag clearly trusted her more. Gwyneth said nothing of this. She merely nodded for Breag to continue.

"The Crones are elusive, as you know," said Sister Breag. "But they are not beyond our reach. We will lure them to the Clochar. I am certain at least one will take the bait and call upon the sisterhood for help."

"That much was already clear to me," said Gwyneth. "Despite the risk."

Franwen's smile broadened. "Yes, it's a calculated risk, but one we must take. The balance must be maintained, and the Crones hold the power."

Gwyneth listened as Breag continued to reveal her plan, a sense of unease growing within her. The beauty of the moonlit temple now seemed shrouded in the shadows of impending decisions and danger. "But even if we manage to capture any of the Crones, how can we possibly keep them here? They're too powerful. Perhaps we could contain one, but the others would surely come for her."

Franwen shook her head. "There is no way to breach the Clochar," she stated firmly. "The Order of Crimson has attempted it numerous times over the centuries, always to no avail. Our defences are unbreakable."

The air in the temple seemed to grow heavier, the weight of centuries bearing down upon them.

Breag nodded in agreement, her eyes gleaming. "And when the other Crones attempt a rescue mission, we will be prepared. They will come to us and make demands. They will play directly into our hands, and we will capture them too."

Gwyneth sighed. "We must not underestimate the Crones," she cautioned. "Their powers are legendary."

Franwen scoffed. "They are novices, new to the magnitude of their abilities. Their inexperience is a liability, more dangerous to themselves than to us."

Gwyneth remained unconvinced, her frown deepening. "But what if they do not seek our aid? What if they choose not to activate the charms Mathilda has entrusted to them?" Her thoughts briefly touched upon Mathilda's safety, a flutter of worry passing through her before she reined it in, focusing instead on the matter at hand.

It was Breag's turn to smile, a look of satisfaction spreading across her features. "Worry not, Sister Gwyneth. Franwen and I have honed our illusions to perfection. We have laid our traps in the Elder Grove where the Crones seek to deepen their magic. They have already been weakened with their greatest fears, and soon they will unwittingly step into our snare, and we will bind them to our will."

The revelation sent a chill down Gwyneth's spine. Illusions were one thing, but to set upon a witch with her own greatest fears was a devious move designed to weaken the spirit and test one's faith in the divine. Such tests were usually reserved for those seeking the role of elder sister and were entered into willingly. To ensnare people without their knowledge or consent was another matter entirely, yet it she could not deny its cunning. Through their terror and despair the Crones would be far more likely to reach for the charms Mathilda had given them. Gwyneth trembled at the lengths the sisterhood would go to ensure a better world...

Breag and Franwen exchanged knowing glances. They did not have faith in Gwyneth's loyalty.

Taking a deep breath, Gwyneth bowed her head in a gesture of deference. "You are wise, Sister Breag, Sister Franwen. I am humbled by the ingenuity of your plan. The Sisterhood shall indeed prevail."

Yet, as Franwen's gaze darkened slightly, and Breag's eyes sparkled with triumph, Gwyneth couldn't help but question the path ahead.

The Veiled Sisterhood's actions were always justified by the pursuit of a greater good. Yet, as the moon cast its silent judgment upon the temple, Gwyneth pondered the true cost of their victory.

51

AGATHA

Agatha's heart pounded in her ears and her stomach dropped at the realisation that she was no longer on solid ground. Beneath her feet, a large cloud had somehow crystallised into a firm surface, but the knowledge that she was suspended in the air, high above the earth, did little to ease her fear of heights.

An island of clouds stretched around her, a surreal landscape bathed in golden light, an unearthly expanse of tranquillity, suspended in the boundless azure sky.

Agatha's breath caught in her throat. This was impossible, yet perfectly wonderful. It was a marvel of nature, where the cloud beneath her had solidified into a firm yet slightly yielding surface, resembling frosted glass while a radiant beacon of light shone out across the island, accentuating the delicate wisps and swirls of the cloud. The edges of the island faded gently into the surrounding air, creating a sense of infinity, as they floated untethered in the vastness of the sky.

"How beautiful!" said Marjie, following Agatha through, as cheerful as usual as if she were admiring a child's painting and not standing miles above the earth.

The dragon puppy yapped happily and followed after her.

"I can't say I'm completely prepared to admire the vista," Ingrid grumbled, looking rather pale. "I'm with Agatha on preferring solid ground in this case."

"Look," said Marjie. "The light's coming from over there."

She gestured to the centre of the cloud island where, indeed, a beacon of golden rays were shining from.

"How does it work?" Agatha asked, cautiously approaching it.

Marjie, always quick to lighten the mood, replied, "Well, Agatha, I don't think it comes with an instruction manual. Maybe try tapping your heels together and wishing?"

"I'll wish for you to grow a better sense of humour," Agatha muttered.

The dragon puppy barked as a dark blue shape opened up before them.

Ingrid had been exploring the edges of the island when she suddenly called out, "Stand back!"

Agatha prepared her magical defences and was ready to launch an attack when Delia stepped through what turned out to be a portal.

"Delia!" Marjie beamed.

Ingrid grimaced. "Where have you been?"

Agatha, recovering from her initial shock, asked sternly, "Where indeed?"

But she was cut off by Marjie who seemed even more awfully cheerful than usual. "Never mind that now. We have to focus."

The crones approached the source of the golden light, gathering around in puzzlement.

"I'm sure this thing is something to do with the air dragon," Agatha said. "We are so close. I'd bet my special sherry decanter on it."

Ethereal light shone out, illuminating the tufts of clouds surrounding them. Agatha's heart quickened with anticipation as she reached out to touch the beacon of light. Her fingertips tingled with the raw energy it emitted.

But as she leaned towards it, a shift occurred in the sky around them. Dark clouds rolled in with alarming speed, shadowing out the once serene vista with their ominous presence. Thunder rumbled in the distance, warning of an impending storm.

The Crones exchanged worried glances.

Marjie's cheerful demeanour faltered, her eyes darting nervously between the turbulent sky and the shining golden light before them. "This doesn't feel right."

Ingrid stepped closer, her hand resting reassuringly on Agatha's shoulder. "We must proceed with caution. Whatever power lies within this light, it seems to have stirred something in the elements."

Delia remained silent, her brow furrowed as she scanned the broody horizon.

Agatha squared her shoulders, undeterred, and focused her attention on the beacon of light once more.

As if responding to her, the light intensified, casting intricate patterns and symbols in the air and cloud around them and beneath their feet.

Agatha stepped forward, her hands outstretched towards the light. She attempted to attune herself to its energy, to decipher the meaning of the patterns, but the symbols eluded her, flickering chaotically in response to her touch. The more she tried, the less sense it made, leaving her frustrated.

Marjie, unable to resist, shook her head with a smile. "Shouldn't you have learnt your lesson to trust your intuition by now, Agatha?"

Delia scoffed, "Agatha has intuition? What is this world coming to?"

Ingrid responded dryly. "Delia, you've missed quite a lot on your mysterious foray into the snow, it seems."

Ignoring their banter, Agatha tried once more to connect with the beacon, squinting in concentration. The symbols continued to swirl around her, their meaning as elusive as ever.

Ingrid cleared her throat. "Focus on your power, Agatha. And listen. Silence is golden."

Agatha closed her eyes, taking a deep breath to calm her racing mind, pushing aside her frustration.

In the silence, she tried to connect with the core of her power, the essence of the element of air. But despite her efforts, the beacon of light remained an enigma, its secrets locked away. The symbols continued to spin and churn, indifferent to Agatha's desires.

Ingrid's voice echoed in her mind and Agatha's senses sharpened, her focus honing in on the pulsating energy emanating from the beacon. With a deep breath, she closed her eyes, shutting out the chaos of the storm raging around her, and delved inward, seeking the core of her power with more determination than ever.

A deafening roar shattered the air. Agatha's eyes snapped open.

There, emerging from the space above the beacon, was an astounding sight that sent shivers down her spine – the air dragon – a magnificent creature, enormous and terrifying. Its form swirled with tendrils of cloud, crackling with the energy of the storm. Its scales sparkled with otherworldly iridescence.

Agatha stood transfixed as the dragon's piercing gaze locked onto hers. She braced herself against the howling wind, her heart pounding in fear and wonder.

As the dragon drew nearer, Agatha's awe gave way to confusion. Its form seemed to waver and shift, like a mirage.

With growing dismay, Agatha realised that the creature before her was not solid – it was composed of air, insubstantial and ephemeral.

Disappointment bloomed in Agatha's chest. This was no ancient beast, it was a mere spectre. Yet, as the air dragon's piercing gaze locked onto hers, the world around her seemed to dissolve, the howling wind fading to a distant whisper. In an instant, the dragon's essence surged forward, enveloping her mind in a vortex of shimmering energy. Agatha felt her consciousness expand, her mind stretching beyond the confines of her physical form, merging with the vast expanse of the universe itself.

In an instant, she found herself standing amidst the towering shelves of an ancient library, the air heavy with the scent of aged parchment and dust. Tomes of forgotten lore beckoned to her, their spines glinting with hidden knowledge. "Behold," the dragon's voice echoed through her mind, "the countless hours you've dedicated to unravelling the mysteries of magic, the unwavering pursuit of wisdom that has defined your life's work."

A sense of deep satisfaction washed over Agatha. It was nice to be recognised, after all. Especially for her years of work, all her historical research and writing, her knowledge.

"Your wit and reason have illuminated the darkest corners of ignorance," the dragon whispered, "shedding light on the wonders of the arcane."

Agatha reached out, her fingers brushing against the weathered covers, and suddenly, the scene shifted. She was transported to a vast auditorium, where eager faces gazed up at her, hanging on her every word as she shared the fruits of her research. The air dragon's presence enveloped her, its voice a whisper in her ear. "Your wit and logic have illuminated the darkest corners of ignorance, sparking the fires of curiosity and understanding in countless minds."

In a blink, Agatha found herself floating amidst the stars,

galaxies swirling around her in a cosmic display of breath-taking beauty. The dragon's voice resonated through the void. "Just as air permeates every corner of the word, so too does knowledge flow through the fabric of existence. Your tireless pursuit of truth has allowed you to grasp the fundamental laws that govern reality and magic itself."

Agatha stared in awe at the billions of stars.

The dragon's voice resonated through the void. "Your mind has soared to new heights, grasping the very fabric of reality, weaving together the threads of existence."

Agatha marvelled at the vastness of the cosmos, feeling the weight of her own insignificance and yet, at the same time, the significance of her life's work. The dragon's essence swirled around her, its voice filled with warmth and wisdom. "Through the power of your mind, you have transcended the limitations of the physical world, soaring on the wings of thought to explore realms beyond the reach of mortal senses."

"Are you ready to go further into the realm of air?" the dragon asked.

"You betcha!" Agatha replied gleefully.

Her mind soared through the realms of knowledge as she found herself transported to a realm of pure thought. The landscape around her shifted, taking on the form of intricate geometric patterns and equations that pulsed with a mesmerising rhythm. The dragon's voice echoed through the space. "Behold, Agatha, the language of the universe itself – the formulas and principles that underlie all of creation."

Agatha gaped at the beauty and elegance of the divine

equations and patterns, feeling a deep understanding wash over her. This was the essence of all life, of divine mythic force, as it swam into being, influencing the worlds, the gods and all beings, all matter, the galaxies, the universe, and all of evolution.

The dragon's presence enveloped her, guiding her through a labyrinth of configurations, paradoxes, and symmetries, revealing the hidden connections that bound seemingly disparate concepts together.

In another instant, Agatha found herself standing on a precipice overlooking a vast expanse. The air dragon's voice whispered in her ear, "Gaze upon the infinite possibilities that lie before you, Agatha. Each decision you make, each path you choose, ripples out across the fabric of reality, shaping the course of your life and the lives of those around you."

The dragon's essence swirled around her, its voice filled with encouragement. "Trust in your wisdom, Agatha, and let it guide you through the challenges that lie ahead. For in the face of uncertainty, it is the strength of your mind and the clarity of your purpose that will light the way."

Agatha found herself immersed in a kaleidoscope of sensations and thoughts, each one a reflection of the deep truths the air dragon was revealing to her. The boundaries of her consciousness expanded, encompassing the entirety of her life's experiences, weaving them together into a masterpiece of unparalleled beauty and meaning.

The dragon's voice echoed through her being. "You are a part of something greater, Agatha – a web of knowledge and understanding that spans the ages. Your contributions, born of your unwavering dedication and the power of your intellect, will resonate through the annals of history, inspiring generations yet to come, but to know your true power you must accept your limitations – to be absolutely meaningful is to accept the shadow – of absolute meaninglessness – to humble yourself in service of the divine totality."

Agatha felt a sense of humility and gratitude wash over her, the true significance of her life's purpose crystallising in her mind. The air dragon's essence enveloped her once more, its voice filled with warmth and pride. "You have walked the path of wisdom, Agatha, and in doing so, you have become a beacon of light in a world often mired in darkness. Embrace both light and darkness and your role as a guardian of knowledge will continue to illuminate the way for those who seek truth and understanding."

As quickly as it had begun, the journey came to an end, and Agatha found herself back on the cloud island, her body trembling with the aftershocks of the incredible experience.

The air dragon hovered before her, its form shimmering like a mirage. "You see, Agatha," it said softly, "the power of air is not insubstantial. It is the breath of inspiration, the wind that carries the seeds of knowledge, the essence of thought itself."

Agatha nodded slowly, her voice tinged with disappointment. "I appreciate all that, but you're just made of air. It's not quite the same as something tangible, is it?"

The dragon's form rippled, as if contemplating her words. "Every elemental dragon is of its element, Agatha, and each element has its own unique gifts. But if you wish for me to become more substantial, we can work together. Teach me the ways of the physical world, and I will learn, for learning is what I do best."

With a gentle swirl, the dragon's essence began to condense, flowing towards Agatha's outstretched hand. "For now, I will stay with you in a simple form of matter," it said, its voice growing fainter, "and you can call upon me as you will."

As the last wisps of the dragon's essence coalesced, a small, golden amulet materialised in the air in front of Agatha. She marvelled at the intricate engravings that adorned its surface, sensing the hum of the dragon's presence within.

As she reached forward to grasp it, the amulet fell. It clattered to the ground, the sound echoing through the stillness of the surreal landscape.

Agatha grumbled as she crouched to retrieve the sacred artifact, but it was more out of habit than grouchiness, and her predominant emotion was still light and free and amazed at the wonders of the universe.

As she picked up the amulet, Agatha's gaze swept across the cloud island, taking in the gleaming tufts of cloud and the ethereal light that bathed the surreal expanse. Everything looked subtly different, as if she was perceiving it with new eyes.

With a smile playing at the corners of her lips, Agatha turned to face her fellow crones, the amulet clutched tightly in her hand.

The pendant was exquisite. At its heart was a stone of vivid golden topaz, pulsating with an inner glow.

Marjie's voice cut through the silence. "Do you think that huge beast is in there?"

"I haven't the foggiest clue," Agatha replied, shaking her head, then looking around, she noticed the sky had cleared and all was serene again. "At least that storm has dissipated."

"How do we get down from here?" Delia asked.

Ingrid chuckled. "We could have ridden Agatha's dragon."

Agatha frowned. "Not bloody likely. I'm not riding the wind. What do you think I am, a seagull?"

"Better a gull than a fool," Marjie muttered under her breath.

Agatha looked down at the pendant in her hand. Just as she began pondering how to coax out the magnificent yet frustratingly insubstantial creature, her thoughts were disrupted by the dragon puppy's bark, followed by a low, defensive growl.

The crones turned their attention towards the western sky, where a dark, fiery shape appeared in the distance, moving swiftly towards them.

"What in the world is that?" Agatha said, her eyes widening with apprehension.

Ingrid gulped. "Whatever it is, it's coming right for us!"

52

DELIA

Delia gasped as the dark shape in the sky swiftly approached. "A dragon!"

"Are you sure?" Ingrid asked, raising her monocle.

"It's reptilian and flying – what else could it be?" Delia asked, noticing a figure in a red cloak riding on the beast, face obscured by a hood. A suspicion ignited within her, fuelling a surge of rage – could it be Jerry? One of his henchmen?

The creature roared and flames burst forth.

"I'd say Delia was right," Marjie muttered.

"Now *that's* a dragon!" Agatha exclaimed with awe and fear in her voice. "None of this vanishing air beast nonsense."

"And it's coming straight for us!" Delia cried out. "Help!"

Delia's hand instinctively reached for her pocket. The charm her grandchildren made her had helped her break through the illusions of the previous night; was there enough magic left to help her now? Or was her firepower all she had? Her fingers grazed against a small leather pouch.

"Ingrid," Delia said. "The sisterhood – they could help us."

Ingrid shook her head and looked at the dragon puppy. "It's time."

The puppy, clearly understanding the gravity of the situation, gazed back at her with solemn, ancient eyes and then swiftly transformed back into her former glory – the magnificent earth dragon.

"Climb aboard!" Ingrid called out to the others. "It's alright."

The crones quickly clambered onto the dragon's back, each finding a secure foothold. As the dragon took to the skies, Delia's heart soared.

Marjie and Agatha both let out cheers of joy.

"This is something I've only ever dreamed about, and probably only as a young child, at that," Delia said, leaning into the wind as the dragon rose higher into the sky. But their shared relief and excitement quickly turned to fear as the other creature swiftly closed in on them.

"Looks like the Order has managed to find a dragon of their own somehow," Marjie said, eyeing the red-cloaked figure with suspicion.

"That's what I was thinking," said Delia. "They've been so quiet recently, I'd rather hoped they'd given up on us...but I was overly optimistic."

"It certainly looks that way," Ingrid said. "But things are not always as they appear."

As Delia clung desperately to the back of the magnificent dragon, the wind whipped fiercely around her, tugging at her clothes and hair with unrelenting force. Below her, the world was a distant blur of colours and shapes far removed from the perilous heights at which they soared. The vulnerability of being so high, so exposed, chilled her to the core.

The earth dragon roared, its voice echoing powerfully across the sky as it swooped.

The enemy creature responded with agility, diving in fast towards them.

"We can't just sit here riding a dragon and twiddling our thumbs," said Agatha. "Let's hit that wily beast with all we've got." She raised her hands and blasted a whirlwind of air towards the creature, which responded by ducking, falling further behind.

"We can do this!" Marjie yelled. "We're crones; we've faced worse than a flying barbecue!"

Delia focussed on her own magic, reaching inside to the furnace of fire, unlocking the gates she usually worked so hard to keep closed, but as she raised her hands to fling flames at the approaching dragon, she lost her grip.

Her heart leapt into her throat as she fell.

She heard Marjie's scream and the wind beating heavily in her ears as she tumbled through the air.

Falling. Falling.

This could not be the end. It was far too silly. What were they going to tell Gilly? That her mother died while falling off a dragon?

Time seemed to slow as she fell; the ground was swiftly rushing up to meet her.

Delia shook herself. Her fire power would be no use now. In panic she reached into her pocket. Her hand brushed against the pouch again; with nothing left to lose, she wrenched open the bag and rubbed the stone.

"Sisterhood! Help!" she cried out.

The stone in her hand pulsed with invisible energy, a last beacon of hope as she plummeted towards the clouds below. Her plea echoed in the vast expanse of the sky...

53
MARJIE

Marjie shrieked in horror Delia fell. It seemed as if time froze, yet the wind whipped fiercely around them, tugging at Marjie's hair and clothes. She barely noticed, her entire focus fixed on Delia, plummeting through the sky.

"Delia!" Marjie cried out.

Agatha and Ingrid followed her gaze and leapt to action, Ingrid directing the earth dragon towards the falling crone, but just as Agatha summoned a small tornado to catch her, Delia vanished into thin air, as if swallowed by the sky itself.

"Oh my goddess!" Marjie blinked, her mind struggling to process what she had just witnessed. Confusion and fear churned within her. Had she just imagined Delia vanishing without a trace? It was too bizarre to be true.

"What just happened?" Agatha asked.

Marjie searched her mind, but before she could grasp any

sane thought, the earth dragon, responding to Ingrid's unspoken command, unleashed a torrent of fire towards the other dragon. The flames enveloped its dark, spiky form, and in an instant, it too vanished.

Ingrid let out a frustrated cry. "Blast! It was nothing but an illusion – a mere trick of light and magic."

"We should have known," Agatha said. "And now Delia is gone...but she didn't hit the ground."

"Where is she?" Marjie asked, her voice trembling slightly.

Ingrid's eyes scanned the skies thoughtfully. "I have my suspicions."

54

DECLAN

eclan sat by the fire. The stew before him simmered gently, its aroma of foraged herbs reflecting the forest's generosity. He ladled a serving into his carved wooden bowl and tasted a spoonful, closing his eyes with pleasure. The flavours were magnified somehow, as if his recent experiences had sharpened his senses too, allowing him to more fully experience the hearty and earthy flavours.

The sun filtered through the canopy, casting dappled light and shadows around him. The forest appeared reborn. Each leaf fluttered like a vibrant heart; each bird call was a soul-quenching song as though he was seeing it all for the first time.

The memory of Delia Spark lingered in his mind, wrapping around him like a warm cloak. Her influence had ignited something within him – a fervour, a zest for life that he'd feared had been permanently decimated under the weight of his immortality. She did not know anything about him, not his age, nor his deepest struggles, yet she knew his soul as he knew hers.

Her touch, her fiery spirit, had sparked a transformation in him. No longer was his eternal life a chain; it was a gift, an opportunity to experience the world anew.

As he savoured his meal he realised that the mundane had become marvellous, the simple had become sublime. Under this new light, to live was not merely to exist but to revel in each moment.

And she set me free...

Declan felt a surge of thrilling liberation. Freed from the constraints of his contract and the oath to serve that had tethered him for centuries.

The forest no longer felt like just a refuge; it was a world alive with possibility interwoven with every leaf, every whisper of wind.

Declan's heart leapt with a newfound liberty, the vibrant midday sun casting his secluded camp in a revelatory light. The fire crackled softly beside him, guarding against the winter chill.

In this moment of solitude, the memory of Delia Spark was both a caress and a conundrum. Yes, she had set him free. Yet, with this came a paradoxical tether: the overwhelming desire to see her again, to be near her. She was mortal, and mortal lives vanished within a blink of the eye of eternity.

The thought of reaching out, of feeling the warmth of her skin, sent a thrill through him, an echo of the euphoria from their intimate encounter.

He reached out to a nearby fern, its fronds soft and cool under his fingertips, and couldn't suppress a smile, giddy with the residue of pleasure that still hummed in his veins.

As he packed away his few belongings, a shadow crept across the brightness of his thoughts. A weight tugged sharply at his heart. Something was wrong – seriously wrong. His gut plummeted.

The forest suddenly seemed too still, too silent.

Declan stood and turned his gaze skyward, mind racing with foreboding. He uttered a single word into the silence: "Delia..."

55

DELIA

Delia slowly opened her eyes, finding herself in a room bathed in bright morning light.

The room was unfamiliar, stark yet comforting, the walls, a pristine white.

Outside, the melodic singing of birds filled the air, harmonious and soothing.

A herby scent, perhaps lavender and sage, lingered in the room, adding to the serene atmosphere.

She sat up, feeling an unexpected sense of peace despite the confusion.

Where was she? The last thing she remembered was falling...falling and reaching into her pocket for...

Her gaze drifted to the doorway where a figure stood – a woman dressed in flowing white garments, her presence calming, almost ethereal.

"Where am I?" Delia asked, with more curiosity than fear.

The woman in white stepped deeper into the room with a deliberate grace. "You are safe here," she said, her voice peaceful and melodious. "You are here in the Clochar. You asked for the sisterhood's help, and we provided."

Delia absorbed her words with a sense of relief washing over her.

The Clochar was a sanctuary, a place of healing and magic. She had been saved by the sisterhood who she had reached out to in her moment of need. The realisation brought a wave of gratitude and a newfound respect for the Veiled Sisterhood.

They had responded to her call, and now, she was in their care, enveloped in the peace and protection of their ancient sanctuary. Now, all was well...

56

EPILOGUE: SABRINA

Sabrina Bracewell sat ensconced in the opulent drawing room. The heavy velvet drapes were pulled back to allow the winter light to seep in, casting long shadows across the Persian rugs and mahogany furniture.

As she sipped her tea with practiced poise, the delicate porcelain barely making a sound upon the saucer, her thoughts wandered to the state of the world beyond these walls — increasingly chaotic and far removed from the order and grace of the old days.

The drawing room, with its high ceilings and walls lined with ancestral portraits, was a mausoleum of the past. Sabrina's gaze lingered on a painting of her great-grandmother, a stern woman who'd wielded magic and influence with an iron fist.

"Those were the days of true power," Sabrina murmured to

herself. "When our family's word was law, both in the mundane and the magical realms."

A frown creased her brow as she considered the fraying edges of her own distinguished family, once as tightly knit as the fine silk tassels adorning the room's grand curtains. Now, those very ties seemed worn.

Her niece, Elamina, in particular, sparked a deep-seated irritation within her – displaying a troubling arrogance in positioning herself as a leader in the political sphere with blatant disregard for the family's legacy and values. And then there was that impostor, Delia Spark, a blight upon the Bracewell legacy.

A sudden cold draft whistled through the room, causing Sabrina to wrap her shawl tighter around her shoulders. It was as if the mansion itself was sighing, weary of the weight of centuries.

Sabrina's ruminations were interrupted by the soft tread of a servant approaching. "A letter has arrived for you, madam," he announced, extending a silver tray upon which lay an unassuming envelope sealed with green wax.

Sabrina took the letter, dismissing the servant with a flick of her wrist.

The seal was familiar, one she hadn't seen in years, and it piqued her interest as much as it heightened her apprehension.

Breaking the seal, she unfolded the letter, her eyes scanning the handwritten lines. It was from an old acquaintance and informant of the magical council for proper conduct – a council of which Sabrina was a longstanding member.

The letter spoke of trouble, of complications involving none other than Delia Spark! Sabrina's shock sent an unwelcome flush to her cheeks, but with a fortifying sip of tea, she returned to her usual state of proper composure and her lips curled into a cunning smile. This was news indeed.

Without delay, she summoned Elamina, who took her time in arriving. However, once she finally presented herself, looking every bit the modern witch in a silver silk suit, Sabrina upheld her composure with regal grace, though she couldn't resist a haughty comment. "Really, Elamina, such an outfit at this hour?"

Elamina, undeterred by her aunt's barbs, cut straight to the matter. "What news do you have?"

Sabrina studied Elamina for a moment, her disdain for the younger woman's attire giving way to a grudging respect for her forthrightness.

Sabrina allowed herself a moment of pause, deliberately increasing the tension in the room. "It seems our dear impostor of a cousin has run into trouble again," Sabrina said. "I've received a message from an informant of the magical council for proper conduct, of which you know I am a lifetime member."

Elamina's expression remained impassive, but her eyes were sharp, attentive. Sabrina revelled in her niece's curiosity but decided not to divulge more than necessary. She did not need to know the letter was from an old acquaintance, Sister Breag. The family's history with the sisterhood, their secrets, and strategies – those were not for Elamina to worry about. Not yet, at least.

"And...?" Elamina prompted, causing Sabrina to narrow her eyes.

"And now," Sabrina continued, a calculated pause drawing out the tension, "I have an errand for you..."

A personal message from Iris

Hello my lovelies! Thank you so much for joining me and the Myrtlewood Crones. If you enjoyed this book, please leave a rating or review to help other people find it!

If you're ready to read more, you can order the next Myrtlewood Crones book, Crone of Mystic Sparks!

If this is your first time reading my books, you might also want to check out the original Myrtlewood Mysteries series, starting with Accidental Magic.

If you're looking for more books set in the same world, you might want to take a look at my Dreamrealm Mysteries series too.

I absolutely love writing these books and sharing them with you. Feel free to join my reader list and follow me on social media to keep up to date with my witchy adventures.

Many blessings,

Iris xx

P.S. You can also subscribe to my Patreon account for extra

Myrtlewood stories and new chapters of my books before they're published, as well as real magical content like meditations and spells, and access to my Myrtlewood Discord community. Subscribing supports my writing and other creative work!

For more information, see: www.patreon.com/IrisBeagle hole

Acknowledgments

A big thank you to all my wonderful Patreon supporters, especially:

Ricky Manthey

Wingedjewels

Elizabeth

Rachel

William Winnichuk

and Danielle Kinghorn

ABOUT THE AUTHOR

Iris Beaglehole is many peculiar things, a writer, researcher, analyst, druid, witch, parent, and would-be astrologer. She loves tea, cats, herbs, and writing quirky characters.

facebook.com/IrisBeaglehole

x.com/IrisBeaglehole

instagram.com/irisbeaglehole

Printed in Great Britain
by Amazon

48531127R00171